THE VANDERBEEKERS

MAKE A WISH

THE VANDERBEEKERS
MAKE A WISH

By Karina Yan Glaser

HOUGHTON MIFFLIN HARCOURT
BOSTON   NEW YORK

hmhbooks.com

Cover design by Catherine Kung
The text is set in Stempel Garamond LT Std.

The Library of Congress Cataloging-in-Publication Data is on file.
ISBN: 978-0-358-25620-5

Manufactured in the United States of America
1 2021
4500831955

To the Glasers and the Dickinsons, who have taught me so much about the meaning of family: Michael, Kathleen, Pat, Larry, Brian, Karen, Josh, Jamie, Dan, Amira, Simon, Eva, Ada, Allie, Caleb, Lucy, Josiah, Kaela, Newell, Selah, Lina, Nora, and Nathan

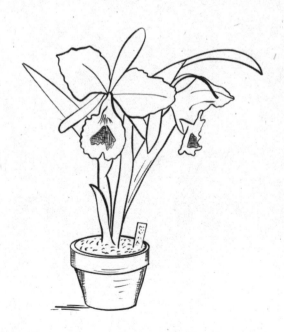

It isn't as if birthdays are common things.
-L. M. Montgomery, *Anne of Green Gables*

In almost everyone's life there is one event that
changes the whole course of his existence.
-E. B. White, *The Trumpet of the Swan*

MONDAY, AUGUST 4

Five Days Until Papa's Birthday

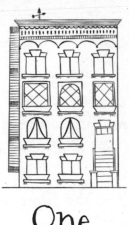

One

*W**ild* was a word that could describe the weather on 141st Street on the first Monday of August. A hot wind rushed through the checkered streets of Harlem with such ferocity that trees bent in wide arches and pedestrians had to lean into the gusts at steep angles to keep from being blown off course. Rain pelted the sidewalks and pooled at street corners. At the top of the red brick brownstone in the middle of the street sat a weathervane that spun so fast it looked as if it might propel the building up into the air and disappear into the clouds.

Down in the basement, Oliver, age twelve and ready to head to the seventh grade next month, was getting ready for a three-day camping trip in the Adirondacks with his dad. Three years ago, when his twin sisters, Isa and Jessie, were in sixth grade, Papa had taken them on a three-day summer getaway trip. His sisters could choose anywhere within driving distance, and they asked to go to Washington, DC. Isa's favorite violinist was performing at the Kennedy Center, and Jessie wanted to go to the Steven F. Udvar-Hazy Center, where the space shuttle *Discovery* was displayed. In the years since then, Oliver had been planning for his summer-after-sixth-grade trip with Papa. And what he wanted to do most was go camping.

Papa and Oliver had researched the best places to camp in the area, and after considering many options, they had decided on the Adirondacks. They had booked a campsite right by a gorgeous lake six months in advance. Oliver had been looking forward to the trip throughout the long, hot, boring summer. And now that the day of departure was finally here, he was in a great mood as he checked the contents of his backpack for the fiftieth time.

Outside, the clouds were low and dark, and wind caused rain to smack against the walls and windows of the brownstone. Upstairs, Mama was finishing up a batch of granola that Oliver and Papa would take with them, the musical clinking of metal bowls and wooden spoons a comforting sound that the Vanderbeeker kids had all been hearing since birth.

In the basement, Laney, who had turned seven that past spring, was observing Oliver while sharing a bowl of crisp red-leaf lettuce with her gray lop-eared rabbit, Paganini.

"This is great lettuce," Laney said as she watched Paganini consume an enormous leaf. "Do you want to bring some on your camping trip?"

Oliver shook his head. "Yuck, no. We're only going to eat junk food. S'mores. Beans right out of the can. Hot dogs."

Franz, a basset hound with long ears that he sometimes stepped on when he sniffed for dropped morsels of food, observed the lettuce-eating with a focus he typically reserved for mealtimes.

"I don't think you're going to like lettuce, Franz," nine-year-old Hyacinth said. She was sewing a plastic cover for Oliver's backpack. He was going to need it with all that rain.

Laney held a piece of lettuce out, and Franz, elated

that food was being handed to him, snatched it from her hand. Then he galloped up the stairs and out of sight.

"I hope he's not hiding that in my bedroom," Oliver commented, looking up from his backpack. "I don't want to find slimy lettuce under my desk when I get back."

A minute later, Franz reappeared and stood in front of Laney, staring at her until she gave him another piece. He disappeared up the stairs again.

"What a weirdo," fifteen-year-old Jessie said.

"Yeah, what a weirdo," Laney echoed.

Isa put down her violin. She'd been practicing a complicated line of music over and over again. "Great," she said to Jessie. "Now Laney's going to be saying that for the next year."

"Weirdo, weirdo, weirdo," Laney said. She liked how the word sounded.

Franz trotted back down the stairs. Laney held out another piece of lettuce to him. He grabbed it, then raced back up the stairs.

"Stop giving him lettuce," Jessie told Laney. "He's going to get sick."

"From vegetables?" Laney asked, popping another piece of lettuce into her own mouth and handing a smaller piece to Paganini. "I doubt it."

"Wild dogs don't eat lettuce," Jessie said. "They're carnivores."

"Franz isn't wild," Hyacinth said. "He could never survive in the wild."

Franz came bounding back down the stairs, lettuce nowhere to be seen. His tongue hung from the side of his mouth, his tail was going at 100 wpm (or wags per minute), and he looked as if he was having the best day of his whole life.

"That dog," Jessie said with a shake of her head. "He's a perfect case study of what fourteen thousand years of domestication will do to you."

The sound of Papa's phone ringing upstairs interrupted their discussion about Franz's heritage. The ringtone was the *Star Wars* theme song, which meant that the caller was Uncle Sylvester, Papa's best friend. Uncle Sylvester and Papa had grown up next door to each other and had even gone to the same college. They both married their college girlfriends right after they graduated, only Papa returned home to Harlem, while Sylvester moved to his wife's hometown in Indiana and became a farmer.

Because Sylvester lived in Elberfeld, a rural part of Indiana, Papa had gone to visit him only twice in the twenty years since college. Sylvester had come to Harlem twice, once to pack up his childhood home and move his parents to Elberfeld (this was before any of the Vanderbeeker kids were born), and once four years ago to visit with his wife, Amelia, and their daughter, Sabine, who was Hyacinth's age. Laney had been a toddler, Hyacinth five years old, Oliver seven, and the twins in fifth grade. The Vanderbeekers immediately loved the family. Sylvester and Amelia had brought them dozens of fresh eggs and bags of vegetables from their farm. It was during their visit that Laney had discovered she hated carrots (and had declared that all orange foods were disgusting) but loved cucumbers, grape tomatoes, and eggplant.

"Uncle Sylvester is calling," Oliver said at hearing Papa's ringtone. Even though Sylvester wasn't technically related to them, they called him "Uncle," since he was like a brother to Papa. "Are you sure you'll get everything done in time for Papa's birthday? You know I can't help for the next few days because of my camping trip."

"We *know* about your camping trip," Jessie said. "You've only mentioned it a million times. We're watching you pack your bag right now."

Papa's fortieth birthday was the coming Saturday, and over the past two months, the Vanderbeekers had been planning a huge surprise party for him. They had invited his friends, even the ones who lived out of town, and the anticipated attendees currently numbered over one hundred. Twenty people were driving in from out of town, and Uncle Sylvester and his whole family were flying in. The Vanderbeekers had planned a day based on Papa's favorite activities and foods.

It had been so hard to plan everything while keeping it a secret from Papa, but the Vanderbeekers had done an excellent job. They could not wait for August ninth.

Isa rubbed her temples. "We still need a present for him."

Oliver sighed.

"Last year when Mama turned forty, we got her a *bakery,*" Laney reminded him.

Papa's Birthday List!
                          CONFIDENTIAL!
-Tour of Yankee Stadium
-Arthur Avenue (pizza and cannolis)
-New York Botanical Garden
-Finale! Birthday Party in Community
                                Garden

   -Bounce House
   -Dancing
   -Papa's Favorite Foods:

      -Spanakopita
      -sushi
      -egg rolls
      -dumplings
      -Greek salad
      -cheese croissants
      -fried chicken
      -cookies

"That was sort of an accident," Hyacinth said.

"An on-purpose accident," Laney added. "We did the best job with her birthday last year."

"He's turning forty," Jessie said. "We *have* to give him a present."

"I thought the *party* was his present!" Oliver said.

Mama's voice drifted down from the kitchen. "Kids, can you come up here, please?"

Oliver, hungry and expecting breakfast, raced up the stairs, and his siblings followed. Their parents were looking at something on Mama's phone.

"Hey, kids," Papa said, then looked at Oliver. "I have some bad news."

"What do you mean?" Oliver said, his eyes growing wide in panic.

"There's been a bit of an emergency," Papa said. "Sylvester's mom passed away this morning. Sylvester needs help with funeral arrangements and asked if I could come out. He's rarely asked me for anything in our entire lives, and I need to go."

"Poor Uncle Sylvester," Hyacinth said.

"Sylvester's mom was like a second mom to Papa when he was growing up," Mama said.

"Really?" Laney asked.

Papa nodded. "After my mom died, it was just me and my dad, and he worked a full-time job. I don't think I could have survived without Sylvester's family."

The Vanderbeekers had never met Papa's parents,

since his mom died when Papa was two and then his dad died when Papa was in college. Papa had shared some stories about his dad, though, and it always made the Vanderbeekers sad not to have known him.

"Not to be insensitive," Oliver said, "but what about our camping trip?"

"I'm so sorry," Papa said to Oliver. "Maybe we can book another campsite for next week?"

"They're all booked until Thanksgiving," Oliver said. "I just checked last night because I wanted to see photos of our campsite. *Everything* is booked."

Papa's face fell. "I'm so sorry, Oliver. I feel terrible."

"How long will you be gone?" Isa asked.

"The funeral is on Wednesday, and I'll fly back on Thursday," Papa replied.

"That stinks!" Oliver said. "You'll be gone the whole time we were supposed to be camping!"

Jessie kicked his foot. "Way to be compassionate, Oliver."

"What?" Oliver said, looking around. "We've been planning this for years!"

Mama put her arm around Oliver. "I'm sorry. I know you're disappointed."

"I will make it up to you, Oliver," Papa said. "I'll look up other campsites. It doesn't have to be at that exact lake."

"We chose that one because it was the best," Oliver grumbled.

"You should go pack," Mama told Papa. "You need to leave in twenty minutes."

While Papa ran up the stairs to his and Mama's bedroom, Mama looked at Oliver in concern. "Are you okay? Maybe we can do something special this week. I wish I didn't have to cover extra shifts, but a couple of my employees are out of town for summer vacation."

"We'll think of something," Isa told her mom. "We don't have plans this week anyway."

"I was going to build the hugest fort in my bedroom," Laney said. "Oliver, you can help."

"Yippee," Oliver said sullenly.

"Are your friends around?" Mama asked. "Maybe you could hang out with them. Have a sleepover in the treehouse?"

"Jimmy L is spending the whole month with his grandparents in Florida." Oliver sighed.

"And Angie is at summer camp in Massachusetts

this month," Hyacinth said. "We said goodbye to her last Saturday."

Before Mama could respond, there was a crash above their heads.

"I think Papa is trying to get the suitcases," Mama said. She glanced at the clock again. "Can you help him pack while I finish getting breakfast ready? He really does have to leave soon if he's going to make his flight."

✿ ✿ ✿

The Vanderbeekers made their way up the stairs, down the hallway, and into Mama and Papa's room. The closet door was open, but Papa was nowhere to be seen.

"Papa? Are you okay?" Laney asked, dropping to the floor and looking under the bed. Tuxedo, their black-and-white cat, darted through the quilt hanging over the edge of the bed, interrupting their other cat, an orange-and-white tabby named George Washington, who had been napping under the bed.

"I'm in—*achoo!*—here!" Papa said from the depths of the dusty closet. "Watch out!"

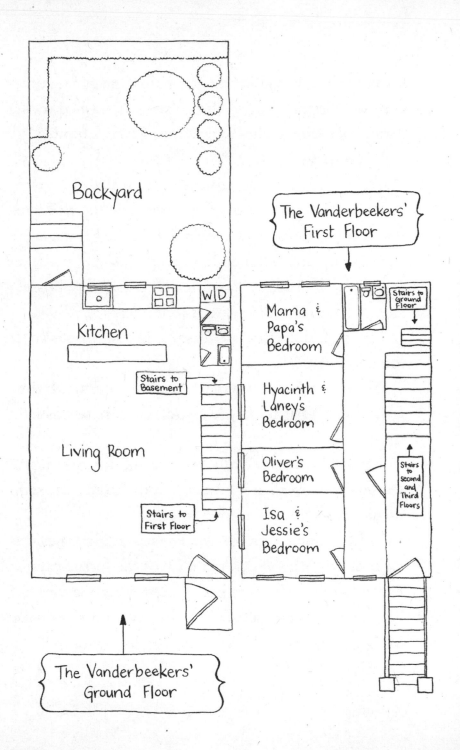

Backyard

The Vanderbeekers'
First Floor

Kitchen

Mama &
Papa's
Bedroom

Stairs to
Ground
Floor

Stairs to
Basement

Hyacinth &
Laney's
Bedroom

Oliver's
Bedroom

Stairs
to
second
and
Third
Floors

Living Room

Stairs to
First Floor

Isa &
Jessie's
Bedroom

The Vanderbeekers'
Ground Floor

W D

There was a rumble before an ancient suitcase tumbled off the top shelf of the closet and crashed to the ground, landing inches away from Laney's head.

"Yikes," Oliver said. "What's that?"

Dusty and old, the suitcase was made of brown-and-orange wool in a plaid pattern. The top and handles were made of brown leather. It looked as if it came out of a movie from the Great Depression.

"This," Papa said, "contains all the earthly possessions I have left from your grandfather."

"How old is that suitcase?" Hyacinth said. "It looks ancient."

"Wait, are you using that thing for your trip?" Jessie asked. "What about the rolling suitcases we usually use?"

Papa picked up the old suitcase and brushed it off, scattering dust all over Laney and Tuxedo. Tuxedo promptly gave an enormous sneeze.

"I lent them to Mr. Jones," Papa said. Mr. Jones was their neighborhood postman. Over the forty years he had worked for the United States Postal Service, he had accrued hundreds of vacation days and was finally using some of them to tour Europe for a month.

"At least I have this," Papa said, holding up the suitcase. "Oliver, can you run downstairs and bring me a cardboard box?"

While Oliver dragged himself downstairs to the basement, where they kept folded-up boxes, Papa unzipped the suitcase, and the Vanderbeekers leaned in to take a look. Scattered inside the frayed silk lining were items of clothing, a few photo albums, and a shoebox.

"What's that?" Laney asked.

"Things that belonged to my dad," Papa said. "This was his suitcase, and I've kept some of his things in here."

Oliver arrived with the box, and Papa transferred all the items into it. The last one was a blazer, plaid again, with thick and thin brown and tan lines interlaced with black lines. The elbows had leather patches thin with wear.

Papa paused for a moment, holding the coat. "He wore this all the time."

"That's so cool," Laney said, reaching out to touch it.

"I wish we had known him," Isa said, looking up at Papa. "I always love hearing stories about your dad."

"He was like the mayor of the neighborhood. Everyone called him Pop-Pop," Papa said.

"He sounds like you," Oliver said, forgetting about his camping disappointment for a moment.

Papa smiled. "Being compared to my dad is the best compliment."

"I'm sorry about Sylvester's mom," Hyacinth told him. "We know she meant a lot to you."

Papa placed his father's blazer on the bed and brought his kids in for a hug.

"She was amazing," Papa said. "She was like your mom, always baking and cooking for other people. My dad was great in so many ways, but he was a terrible cook! I spent a lot of evenings eating dinner at Sylvester's house."

"What time is your flight?" Jessie asked, looking at her watch. "It's nine o'clock now."

"Shoot," Papa said. "I've got to leave in five minutes."

The Vanderbeeker kids rushed around grabbing Papa's toiletries and throwing T-shirts and jeans and socks and a phone charger into Pop-Pop's ancient suitcase, each item causing a puff of dust to billow up. Papa tossed in underwear and dug out his fancy pair of shoes from the far corner of the closet while Isa put in a book. The packing finished, Oliver zipped up the luggage and Papa pulled out the one nice suit he owned and draped it over his arm. It was already enclosed in a garment bag.

"I think I'm ready," Papa said at the same time Mama called up the stairs, "Honey, you should get going!"

They went downstairs and watched Papa tie his sneakers and grab his wallet, keys, and phone and shove them into his jacket pocket.

"I love you all," Papa said, opening the door. He looked at Oliver once more. "And I'm really sorry, Oliver. I'll make it up to you."

"Be safe out there," Mama said, looking outside. The wind was fierce.

"The wind is supposed to let up in an hour," Jessie noted, looking at the weather on her phone.

"Good," Hyacinth said. She didn't like thinking about Papa on a plane in this weather.

After hugging Mama and all the kids, Papa picked up the suitcase, and the Vanderbeekers followed him to the sidewalk in front of the brownstone.

Oliver watched him walk down the sidewalk to the avenue, where he could hail a taxi, already feeling as if the brownstone was lonelier and emptier without him.

Two

Come on," Mama said, ushering the kids back inside the brownstone. "Let's get some breakfast."

"We were supposed to be leaving for our camping trip right now," Oliver said forlornly.

"How about I make you my super-special cheese, egg, and tomato sandwich?" Mama said, putting an arm around him.

"And afterward you can take me bike riding!" Laney added. She had just learned how to ride a bike without training wheels, but unfortunately, her bike was so small that her knees hit the handlebars with every rotation. Since Hyacinth was still using her bike, Laney couldn't move up to a bigger bike yet. Nevertheless, Laney was able to ride admirably, despite looking as if she belonged in the circus.

While Mama finished getting breakfast ready, the Vanderbeeker kids (except Oliver, who moped on the couch) set the table and filled glasses with water for Jessie and Isa, milk for Laney and Hyacinth, and juice for Oliver. Jessie brewed a cup of ginger tea for Mama. Isa donned oven mitts to remove the casserole from the oven, and Mama sliced into the crackly crust of a fresh loaf of sourdough. She got Oliver's special sandwich ready and placed the rest of the sourdough slices on a platter with butter and jam. Jessie brought the platter to the table, and everyone sat down.

Jessie glanced at Papa's seat, sending up a silent prayer that he would have safe travels to Indiana. She remembered her first and only plane trip, which had happened last year when she and Mr. Beiderman, their third-floor neighbor, flew to Atlanta to find Jessie's best friend, Orlando. Now Orlando lived with Mr. Beiderman, and after nearly nine months of filling out forms, Mr. Beiderman had received final approval to be Orlando's legal guardian.

Mama blessed the food, and everyone except Oliver made a grab for the sourdough.

"Will Uncle Sylvester still be able to come to Papa's birthday party?" Laney asked.

"I'm not sure," Mama said. "I guess we'll know later this week. Jessie, can you get my phone? I think it's in the bedroom. I need to double-check my work schedule."

Jessie went upstairs and stepped inside her parents' bedroom. It smelled so good in there, like fresh linens and lavender. She grabbed Mama's phone from the bedside table, and as she was leaving, Pop-Pop's blazer, which was still on the bed, caught her eye. Slipping Mama's phone into her pocket, Jessie picked up the blazer. She was about to place it in the cardboard box holding Pop-Pop's other possessions when she had the overwhelming desire to put it on.

She slipped her right arm into the sleeve, the worn silk lining cool and reassuring against her arm. She reached her left arm back to slip the other sleeve on, and while it was slightly large, the blazer settled itself onto her body as if it was made for her. Pop-Pop must have been the same height and build as Papa. Jessie had passed her mom in height last year, then sprouted another few inches in the last couple of months. She was now getting close to her dad's height, and nearly every day, one of her neighbors commented on this fact.

Jessie opened the closet and looked into the mirror that hung on the inside of the door. The jacket made her look a lot like Papa, and that made her happy. She ran her fingers along the shell buttons and the slightly scratchy wool fabric and the smooth leather of the elbow patches. Her grandfather had worn this blazer hundreds of times, and somehow it made her feel connected to him in a way she had never experienced before. She kept the blazer on and went back down the stairs. She found Laney trying to circle the dining room table on her tiny bike while Tuxedo, George Washington, and Paganini sought refuge under the couch and Franz ran after Laney, barking.

"Whoa," everyone said when they saw Jessie.

Laney hopped off her bike and ran to Jessie for a closer look.

"It fits you!" Isa said.

"It's a little big," Jessie said, holding her arms out.

"You look just like Papa in that jacket," Laney observed.

"She looks just like *Pop-Pop* in that jacket," Mama said. "Wait a second. *Is* that Pop-Pop's jacket?"

Jessie nodded. "It was in the suitcase Papa used for his trip."

"Wow," Mama said. "I haven't seen that in years. Pop-Pop wore that all the time."

"It feels really good to wear," Jessie said, hugging the jacket around her before sitting back down at the table. "Like I know him somehow."

Mama teared up a little bit. "I wish you had known him. He had a smile that lit up a room. I think about him all the time."

"How did he die?" Oliver asked.

Mama looked at her kids in surprise. "Papa never told you?"

They shook their heads.

"It was the day before Papa's college graduation," Mama began. "We were so excited he was coming to the ceremony, especially since his health hadn't been great earlier that year. When we talked to him that morning, he sounded really happy. But then Papa got a call that night. Pop-Pop had had a heart attack. He died on the way to the hospital."

"That is so sad," Hyacinth said. "Poor Papa!"

"It was terrible," Mama said. "We flew back to New York City right away."

"Papa didn't go to his college graduation?" Jessie asked.

Mama shook her head.

"Wow," Isa said. "I had no idea. He never said anything about that before."

"He doesn't like talking about it," Mama said, then glanced at the clock. "I've got to get to the bakery. Can you clean up after you're done eating?"

The Vanderbeeker kids nodded and started to clear the table while Mama grabbed her bag and dashed out the door.

As they loaded the dishwasher with their breakfast plates, Hyacinth spotted movement outside the living room window that faced out onto 141st Street. It looked as if someone was bringing lots of bags right to their door.

Wondering who could have ordered so many packages, Hyacinth walked to the living room window and pulled back the curtain.

"Um, Isa?" Hyacinth said. "You should come see this."

Isa made her way to the window and peered outside.

"Oh no," she said, replacing the curtain as the door-bell rang.

"What's going on?" Oliver asked.

"Isa? Jessie? Open up!" came a voice from behind the door.

The Vanderbeeker kids looked at one another.

"Did *you* know they were coming?" Oliver asked Isa.

"Don't you think I would share that information?" Isa replied, panicked.

Jessie was hurriedly texting their mom.

"I know you're home! I saw you through the win-dow!" came the voice on the other side of the door.

Jessie's phone pinged. "Mama says, 'Seriously? I'm so sorry! Take care of them until I get home, please!'"

"This day could not get any worse," Oliver muttered.

"I'm opening the door," Isa said, her hand on the handle. "Everyone ready?"

"No," said Jessie, Oliver, Hyacinth, and Laney.

"Grab Franz," Isa said before opening the door. A gust of wind whooshed into the brownstone, and Franz howled and strained at his collar as Hyacinth tried to pull him back.

"Took you long enough," the woman outside said. She held a gigantic umbrella. Her hair was combed up and out to make her look as if she had been electrocuted, and she wore a silk shirt with black pants and leather pumps. A pearl necklace draped around her neck. Standing next to her was a man wearing a white button-down shirt, slacks, and black shoes that looked like the ones Papa wore to church.

"Why are you still in your pajamas at this hour?" the woman asked Isa, her mouth pressed into a firm frown. "And what happened to your hair? You have such beautiful hair and don't even brush it." The woman looked at Jessie, then raised her voice to be heard over Franz's barking. "What on earth are you wearing? Is that a man's jacket? What a horrible color. Hyacinth! I see you hiding behind Isa. Come out so I can get a look at you. Can't you lock up that horrid dog?"

The man next to her didn't say a word, but he took a hasty step back when Franz lunged toward him in an attempt to lick his hands.

Isa opened the door wider and swallowed. "Hi, Grandma. Hi, Grandpa. How nice to see you."

Three

Isa stared at her grandparents. "So . . . what are you doing here?"

Grandma tsked and stepped inside. "Didn't your parents tell you we were visiting? Aunt Penny came with us. She's bringing all the bags."

"Aunt Penny!" exclaimed Laney. She ran past her grandparents, leaped over the pile of luggage stacked on the doorstep, and dashed out into the rain.

Aunt Penny was mom's cousin; Grandma and Aunt Penny's mom were sisters. Penny lived in California and visited the Vanderbeekers every year, although usually around Thanksgiving. She called frequently and always remembered their birthdays.

Isa, Jessie, Oliver, and Hyacinth were left with the grandparents. There was an uncomfortable moment as they stared at one another. Behind their grandparents was a mountain of wet luggage. Beyond that, on the sidewalk, was Aunt Penny. She was standing next to a taxi-sized suitcase and hugging Laney.

"Hi!" Aunt Penny called when she caught sight of Isa. She brushed wet hair out of her eyes. "Any chance you can help me drag this into your apartment? I think your grandma brought every pair of shoes she owns!"

"I can help!" Laney exclaimed. She grabbed a handle, pulled as hard as she could, and budged the bag not one inch.

Isa picked up an umbrella and hopped over the luggage heap with Oliver to lend a hand. She gave Aunt Penny a hug and handed her the umbrella, and Isa and Oliver each seized a handle of the duffel, letting Aunt Penny shake out her tired arms.

"I'm so glad to see you!" Aunt Penny exclaimed, huddled under the umbrella.

"We're glad to see you too," Isa said, grunting as

she and Oliver dragged the duffel toward the front door. "We weren't expecting you!"

"Seriously?" Aunt Penny said. "Your grandparents have been planning this trip for a month. I, on the other hand, just found out I had some vacation time I had to use or else they would take it away. My mom mentioned that your grandparents were visiting for your dad's birthday, so I figured I'd surprise you. I guess it worked!"

"*You* were a good surprise," Laney said, hugging her aunt again.

"No one told us," Oliver said. "Grandma has already insulted Isa's hair and told Jessie that her jacket was ugly."

Aunt Penny stifled a smile. "If you're looking to compare who had it worse with your grandma, let me tell you that on the bus ride up here, she advised me to wear makeup and better clothes so I could attract a husband. Then she sent a text to all of her friends with a photo of me that she had 'made better' with a filter and asked if they knew of any single doctors or lawyers who were looking for a wife."

"You win," Isa and Oliver said at the same time.

"She's a character," Aunt Penny said.

"I was supposed to be on a camping trip with Papa right now," Oliver said. "But his best friend's mom passed away, and now Papa is at the airport waiting for a flight to Indiana."

"Oh, that's terrible, Oliver," Aunt Penny said. "I'm sorry about your camping trip. That stinks."

"We're glad you're here, though," Laney said.

"I can't believe you didn't know we were coming," Aunt Penny said. "Your mom didn't say anything?"

Isa and Oliver shook their heads.

"Usually she's so organized," Aunt Penny said, watching Laney leap over the luggage and head into the brownstone. "I can't imagine she would forget."

The luggage was now all at the doorway, and Isa and Oliver again made their way over the pile of bags and started dragging things into the apartment.

Inside, their grandma was scolding their youngest sister.

"Your shirt is backward and inside out!" Grandma said.

"It's more comfortable that way," Laney explained. "The tag itches my neck."

Grandpa just stood by silently, looking as if he would rather be at the dentist's.

Grandma turned her attention to Hyacinth. "Hyacinth, stop hiding behind Jessie! I want to get a good look at you."

At the sound of his favorite human's name, Franz ran toward Grandma to see what she wanted. Grandma shrieked and stepped back to avoid him, and before anyone could say "axelotl," she slipped and crashed to the ground, hitting her head against the lowest stair.

"Grandma!" Laney yelled, and everyone rushed to surround her.

"Is she dead?" Hyacinth asked, horrified.

"She got knocked out," Jessie said. "Give her space."

Everyone except Grandpa took a big step back. Jessie checked for a pulse while Grandpa grabbed her hand and squeezed it. Ten seconds passed.

"This isn't good," Oliver said quietly. "We killed Grandma."

Then Grandma's eyes fluttered open, and Laney yelped in surprise.

"What are you all doing?" Grandma said, trying to sit up.

Jessie helped her to a sitting position. "You hit your head on the step and went unconscious for a few seconds. Hyacinth, get an ice pack."

"I hope you didn't get a concussion," Aunt Penny said, looking over Jessie's shoulder.

Oliver looked for the spot where she had slipped. A greenish blob was smeared on the ground by the stairs. "I think she slipped on the lettuce that Franz spit out earlier today."

"Ew, gross," Laney said, making a face.

Isa ran to the kitchen and grabbed a paper towel to clean it up. "You're right, Oliver. It was the lettuce."

The Vanderbeeker kids turned to look at Franz. He was sitting in front of the living room window, totally unrepentant, his eyes trained on a squirrel running along a branch of the oak tree that grew in front of their brownstone.

"We should go to the emergency room to get an CT scan," Jessie said, turning back to Grandma. "Just in case. Sometimes the brain can hit the inside of the skull and be bruised. There could be bleeding or swelling."

"No," Grandma said. "My brain is fine."

"Yes," Grandpa said, and the Vanderbeekers looked at him in surprise. Was that the first word he had said since he arrived?

"I hate the hospital," Laney said.

"Grandma, just a quick visit," Jessie assured her.

None of the Vanderbeekers were thrilled to go to the hospital. It was at the hospital where they had received the news that Mr. Jeet, their beloved neighbor, was dying. Ever since, they had purposely stopped walking by there, even changing their route to avoid passing it. But Grandma had hit her head pretty hard, and Jessie made an executive decision that they had to leave for the hospital immediately. Grandma must have realized that it was pointless to argue and let Jessie help her up off the floor. Jessie took off Pop-Pop's blazer, hung it on a coat hook, and grabbed an umbrella.

"Who is going to bring in our luggage?" Grandma demanded.

Jessie ignored her and opened the door. Miraculously, Orlando was coming home from a run with

Mr. Beiderman. They were dripping wet from the rain.

"Hey, guys! We have to take Grandma to the emergency room," Jessie said.

"Grandma slipped on slobbery lettuce and hit her head!" Laney reported.

"I'm fine," Grandma hollered from inside the brownstone.

"Can we help?" Orlando asked.

Jessie nodded, then pointed at the luggage. "Can you bring the rest of this in and dry it off? You know where the spare towels are."

"Sure," they said.

Mr. Beiderman waved at Aunt Penny, whom he had met a few times from her previous visits.

"I'm Orlando," Orlando said. He had not met Aunt Penny before. "Nice to meet you."

"Nice to meet you," Penny said, reaching over the bags to shake his hand. "I'm Penny. Cousin to their mom." She tilted her head toward the Vanderbeekers.

"Don't mind me, I just have a medical emergency," Grandma said loudly, then turned to Orlando and Mr. Beiderman. "Be careful with those bags."

"Yes, ma'am," Orlando said, pulling out his Southern charm. He winked at Jessie.

"At least someone has manners around here," Grandma grumbled.

Orlando and Mr. Beiderman stepped inside and moved some bags so there was a pathway for Grandma, Grandpa, and Aunt Penny to go past.

"Thank you!" they said.

"Are you okay walking several blocks, Grandma?" Isa asked when they got to the sidewalk. It was still windy, but at least the rain had slowed to a drizzle. "We could get a cab if that would make you feel better."

"Of course I can walk," Grandma said. "I didn't break my legs."

Isa raised her eyebrows, but she led the way to the hospital. It was a quiet walk, since Grandma was short-tempered. Whenever someone asked if she was okay, she would snap, "Why wouldn't I be?"

When they arrived at Harlem Hospital, Laney refused to go through the doors. When Jessie tried to make her go inside, Laney began to cry.

"I don't want to go in there!" Laney said.

Grandma looked disapprovingly at Laney.

"It's fine," Isa said. "I can stay out here with her. Jessie, can you bring Grandma in?"

"Can I stay outside too?" Hyacinth asked.

"Me too?" Oliver said.

Grandma huffed. "*I'm* going inside!" She walked toward the door, not looking back to see if anyone was following her.

"I'll go!" Jessie said. "Grandma! Wait!" She jogged to catch up, followed by Grandpa and Aunt Penny. Grandma had already disappeared through the automatic glass doors.

Isa took out her phone. "I'm going to call Mama." Her siblings leaned in to listen.

"Hi, Mama," Isa said.

"Hi, Mama!" Laney and Hyacinth said.

"Hey, kiddos. Wow, I can't believe they're here," Mama said.

"Yeah. They brought a mountain of luggage," Isa said.

"How did I not know they were coming today?

Grandma said they were coming *next* weekend for Papa's birthday."

"Also, Grandma hurt her head," Isa added.

Laney leaned toward the phone and yelled into the microphone. "She slipped on lettuce that Franz spit out!"

Isa nudged Laney away from the phone.

"What?" Mama said. "Who spit on her? And what happened with her head?"

"She fell and hit it on the bottom stair. We're at Harlem Hospital now," Isa said. "Jessie, Aunt Penny, and Grandpa went in with Grandma, and now we're just waiting outside. She's probably fine, but we thought we should have a doctor look at it just in case."

"Good thinking. I'll be there in twenty minutes. Hang tight."

Isa put her phone back into her pocket and looked at her siblings, then at the hospital. "Here we are again."

Hyacinth looked at Isa with worried eyes. "Grandma and Grandpa aren't going to stay for longer than just today, are they?"

"Please, no," Oliver said. "That would be awful."

"Maybe they can leave Aunt Penny," Laney said hopefully. "She's fun."

"Be nice," Isa said, even though she secretly agreed with her little sister.

"But Grandma is so mean!" Oliver protested. "It's like she can't say anything nice to us. Remember when Mama showed her that video of you playing at Carnegie Hall, and all Grandma said was the dress you wore didn't look good on you and you should have practiced more?"

"That didn't bother me that much," Isa said. But it *had* bothered her. She had practiced her violin day and night for months in preparation for that concert. She had felt good in her dress and had actually been pretty happy with her performance, which was a rare occurrence. And then Grandma had said those things, and the memory of that performance had soured in Isa's mind.

"I think she means well," Isa said, trying to be objective.

"Yeah, if meaning well involves making us feel bad

about ourselves," Oliver muttered. "Do you think they're going to stay *all* week?"

"I'm sure they just got Papa's birthday confused and they'll come back next weekend," Isa said, silently praying that it would be true.

Four

Jessie was ready to pull her hair out. Grandma was driving her nuts.

"When will that doctor come?" Grandma asked for the sixteenth time in four minutes. "Go ask someone when the doctor will come," she told Jessie.

"I already asked someone five minutes ago," Jessie told her.

"I'll see what's going on," Aunt Penny interjected, and headed off in the direction of the coffee shop.

Grandpa stood there, squinting at the warning label of an IV drip machine that had been abandoned nearby.

Grandma sat on a narrow hospital bed in a corner of the emergency room. Because the hospital was particularly busy, she had to share the tiny curtained-off area with another patient. And that patient *really* liked talking about the various ailments she had.

"When I was twenty," the other patient said, "I was minding my own business, just walking to the bodega to buy some cornflakes, when *wham!* A bike came *barreling* down the sidewalk and knocked me clean over! I was too stunned to see who it was, but Stuart Simon, you know, that nice fellow from the barbershop? He just happened to be walking by at that *exact moment*, and not only did he get a good look at the biker, but *he ran after him*—Stuart ran track in college, you know—and ended up catching up to him! And do you know who had run me over? Mr. Butterfield! Everyone said, 'No, Mr. Butterfield couldn't have done it! He's such a *nice* man! He works at the Seafood Palace!' But it was indeed Mr. Butterfield. He was charged with *reckless biking*."

"I didn't know reckless biking was a thing," Jessie said.

"Mr. Butterfield's bike was the cause of this bump on my heel, from the bone that got knocked out of place. Do you want to see it?"

"No, thank you," Jessie said. Grandma and Grandpa remained silent.

"My cousin Nestor tried to fix it, but I think he made it worse."

"That's nice you have a doctor in the family," Jessie said.

"Nester's not a doctor, but he watches a lot of medical shows. But that bump on my heel in no way compares to the *bunions* on my feet. Those hurt like the dickens, I tell you. I *cannot* find a shoe that doesn't hurt my bunions—"

The metal sliders of the curtain screeched, and a nurse appeared with a clipboard.

"Took you long enough," Grandma snapped at the sight of the nurse.

"Nurse Higgins!" the other patient exclaimed as her eyes lit up.

Nurse Higgins smiled at Grandma. "I'm here for my friend Ms. Peters here. She is a frequent visitor, am I right?"

"That's right!" Ms. Peters said with a big smile.

"What can I help you with today? Earache? A mysterious bump on your stomach? Bunions?" Nurse

Higgins asked with a wink at Jessie, reaching behind her to close the curtain with an efficient snap.

"I've got this strange tickle," Ms. Peters said, pointing at her throat. "I think a fish bone got stuck."

While Ms. Peters explained her condition in vivid terms to Nurse Higgins, Jessie turned back to Grandma. She caught her wincing as she tried to rearrange herself to a more comfortable position on the bed.

"I'll check on the doctor again," Jessie said, stepping toward the curtain and running right into a doctor who was entering.

"Oops!" the doctor said, adjusting her glasses, which had gone askew in the collision. "It's such tight quarters around here!"

Jessie inspected the doctor. The lanyard around her neck had a card dangling at the end of it that said DR. CALLIE. She looked about the same age as some of the kids in Jessie's high school. Her long brown hair was pulled into a ponytail, and her nails had purple polish on them.

"What can I do for you today?" Dr. Callie asked as she rolled in a computer on a narrow black table, wedging it between the two hospital beds and effectively trapping poor Nurse Higgins next to a very animated Ms. Peters. Grandpa peered over Dr. Callie's shoulder at the computer, his thick glasses slipping down his nose.

Grandma sighed heavily. "I explained it four times already."

Dr. Callie looked at the computer screen. "Just one more time for me."

"I fell and bumped my head," Grandma said. "And I'm fine. My granddaughter dragged me here." She glared at Jessie.

"She went unconscious for seventeen seconds," Jessie said.

"What caused the fall?" Dr. Callie asked as she typed furiously on the computer.

Grandma didn't say anything.

"She slipped on mushy lettuce," Jessie said.

"*Romaine* calm, everyone," Dr. Callie said, holding up her hands as if she were a police officer directing traffic. "We'll get this fixed up right away."

Jessie, Grandma, and Grandpa stared at her.

"You know, *romaine*, like the lettuce?" Dr. Callie said, grinning. "Can you point to the part of your head that was hit?"

Grandma gestured, and Dr. Callie parted Grandma's hair to take a look. "There's definitely a bump." She pulled a cold pack out of her medical coat, twisted it, and shook it. "Hold this there for now."

"I think she should get checked for concussion," Jessie said. "She told me she has a headache, but she doesn't have any ringing in her ears, nausea, vomiting, or blurry vision."

Dr. Callie looked at Jessie with appreciation. "Have you ever thought of being a doctor?"

Jessie shook her head. "I want to be a rocket engineer."

"Ah, well," Dr. Callie said. "You don't have to make a decision at this exact moment."

"Can I leave yet?" Grandma called from her bed.

Dr. Callie looked back at her computer. "I need to do some neurological and cognitive testing first. *Lettuce* head to an examination room!"

Grandma groaned.

"Don't worry, it won't *kale* you!" Dr. Callie said.

"Bye!" called Ms. Peters from the other bed. "I hope it's not a tumor!"

Dr. Callie unlocked the wheels of the hospital bed and rolled Grandma down the hallway, and Jessie was surprised that the walk was slow and calm versus the medical shows where the patient was wheeled on a gurney at top speed with dozens of medical professionals racing beside it shouting, "Code blue!" Dr. Callie meandered through the halls, stopping to fist-bump various people in scrubs and saying, "Lettuce through!" then chuckling to herself.

After many winding corridors, they arrived at a hallway with rooms on each side.

Only one person was allowed inside the examination room with Grandma, and since Grandpa had already followed them in, Jessie waited outside. She was about to text Isa to ask how things were going when she heard her mom's voice.

Jessie swiveled to find Mama speed-walking toward her. She still had her work apron on, complete with chocolate stains. Flour dusted her nose and hair.

"I'm so glad you're here," Jessie said.

"How's Grandma?" Mama asked.

"I think she's fine. I mean, she's *super* grouchy, but that's nothing new."

Mama rubbed her temples. "What a mess. Papa's out of town, Grandma might have a concussion, Oliver's trip was ruined, and most of my employees are on vacation."

Jessie put an arm around her mom. "Grandma is fine; I'm certain of it. I mean, she was still giving everyone a hard time when she was waiting for the doctor. I would be more worried if she had been quiet."

Mama laughed, then put a hand over her mouth. "I shouldn't be laughing, but it's so true. One time I got her so mad that she stopped talking to me for—"

Mama stopped abruptly. Jessie let a moment go by before she prodded. "What?"

Mama sighed. "Well, I know what you mean. We had—have—a . . . complicated relationship."

Jessie waited.

Mama tried again. "Let's just say that in all the ways Pop-Pop was warm and loving and accepting, my parents were the opposite. You probably see that in how she treats you."

Jessie nodded. "Has she always been like that?"

"Yes," Mama said. "My parents sacrificed a lot for me and your uncle Arthur. In return, they wanted us to be successful: doctors and lawyers and accountants."

"But you have the best jobs." Her mom ran her own bakery and Uncle Arthur owned a construction business.

Mama smiled. "I do have the best job, and I have you and your siblings to thank for it."

"How long do you think Grandma and Grandpa will be here?" Jessie asked.

"They don't like taking time off from work, so they'll probably leave tomorrow."

"I don't even remember the last time they visited us," Jessie said. "I wish Papa were here."

"Me too."

They stood there, watching the hospital bustle around them. Jessie thought about her grandparents and then, in that weird way that brains have of meandering to various thoughts, about Papa's parents.

"Hey!"

Jessie and Mama turned to find Aunt Penny walking toward them, balancing two cups of coffee.

"Penny!" Mama said. They hugged awkwardly, given the coffee; then Penny handed Mama the extra cup. "What are you doing here? And how did you know I needed coffee right now?"

"I thought I'd tag along on your parents' trip," Aunt Penny said. "As for the coffee, I bought two cups of coffee for myself, but I'm happy to share."

"You've got to kick that coffee habit," Mama told her as she took a sip.

"Hey, I'm on California time!" Aunt Penny said. "My mom told me that your parents were visiting, and I thought I would tag along as a surprise. And of course, I had to be here for Derek's big birthday. I had no idea your parents didn't tell you they were coming."

"It's so strange," Mama said. "They never said a *word* about coming this week."

"Drink up," Aunt Penny said, gesturing to the coffee. "It looks like you could use it."

The door to the examination room opened, and Dr. Callie reappeared, rolling Grandma on the stretcher. Grandpa followed.

"Why do I need this stretcher? My legs work just fine," Grandma grumbled. Then she spotted Mama. "Oh, it's you."

"Hi, Mom. Hi, Dad," Mama said, leaning down to kiss Grandma's cheek. She gave Grandpa a hug.

"You must be her daughter," Dr. Callie said to Mama. "Wow, three generations right before my eyes! How special!"

"Took you long enough to get here," Grandma said, narrowing her eyes at Mama. "I have a teenage doctor diagnosing me."

Jessie wasn't sure if Grandma was referring to her or Dr. Callie.

"What's the news?" Aunt Penny asked.

"Well," Dr. Callie said as she pushed the hospital bed back down the hallway, "my tests show that she's fine, but I would like all of you to keep an eye on her for twenty-four hours. Here's an information sheet for what to look out for. Bring her back if you see anything."

"I told you I was fine," Grandma snapped. "All this fuss for nothing."

"Jessie did the right thing," Mama said. "It's always good to have things checked out."

"It's that dog's fault," Grandma said. "Hyacinth's disgusting dog."

"Franz is a great dog," Mama said sharply to Grandma, then looked at Dr. Callie. "Thank you."

"She should have a follow-up with her general doctor in the next few days," Dr. Callie said.

"They go back home to Ottenville tomorrow," Mama said. "I'll watch her tonight, and we'll make sure she sees her primary care doctor when she goes home."

"Who said I'll be gone by tomorrow?" Grandma demanded.

Mama looked at Grandma in surprise. "You've never stayed more than one night before. I actually had no idea you were even coming today."

"I *said* we were coming to Derek's birthday party," Grandma told her.

Mama's eyebrows furrowed. "Derek's birthday isn't for five days. Anyway, don't you have to get back to work?"

"We took the week off," Grandma said with a shrug.

"*A week?*" Mama said. "I don't remember you taking that much time off . . . ever. Not for a vacation, not when Dad broke his leg, not for my college graduation."

"We wanted to see you," Grandma said simply.

"Does that mean you're staying at our place *all week*?" Jessie blurted out.

Grandma looked at her as if that were the most ludicrous question in the world. "Of course we are. What did you expect?"

Five

Laney was sitting with Hyacinth on the sidewalk outside the hospital, people-watching. The hospital was right by the subway, and they were making up stories about the people coming up the stairs.

"That person," Laney said, pointing to a woman holding a potted plant with huge jungle leaves, "and her plant, Ambrosia, are going to their favorite park to feed the pigeons. They've done that every Monday for the past five years."

"And the woman carrying the duffel bag with the *Hamilton* logo," Hyacinth said, not pointing because she knew that was rude, "is in charge of all of the costumes at the musical. She was up all night sewing a new pair of pants for the guy who plays Thomas Jefferson because he got holes in the knees. Again."

"She gets so annoyed with Thomas Jefferson," Laney agreed. "He can't keep his clothes clean."

Laney was just about to comment on a man riding a bike with a huge stereo tied to the back rack when Jessie came out through the hospital doors with their grandparents, Aunt Penny, and Mama.

"Grandma's fine," Jessie announced. "We have to watch her today, though."

"No, you do not," Grandma said, glaring at her.

"Yes, we do," Jessie said, glaring back.

Mama cleared her throat and checked her watch. "It's noon. I've got to get back to the bakery, but why don't you go home and get your grandparents some lunch?" Then Mama looked at Jessie. "Thank you for keeping an eye on Grandma today. Aunt Penny and Grandpa can help. You can put all their luggage upstairs in my bedroom, since they'll be here all week."

Hyacinth and Laney gasped.

Oliver exclaimed, "All week!" When he saw Grandma's face he added, "That's . . . great news."

"I want to go home with you," Mama said to the

kids, "but I'm too short-staffed at the bakery. We've gotten so many big orders for wedding receptions."

"We'll take good care of her," Isa said.

Laney saw her big sisters exchange a look. Suddenly, that feeling when something was about to go very, very wrong filled her stomach.

✻ ✻ ✻

When they returned to the brownstone, Isa and Jessie made lunch for everyone while Aunt Penny peppered Grandma with questions from Dr. Callie's information sheet. This made Grandma even more ornery, and she retaliated by berating the kids all through lunch. When Aunt Penny suggested that Grandma lie down for a nap, they were all surprised when she agreed without an argument. The Vanderbeeekers gave a collective sigh of relief.

"I'll get them settled," Aunt Penny said as she led Grandma and Grandpa up the stairs.

Hyacinth was glad to be away from her grandparents for a little bit. She sat on the couch petting Franz and watched as Jessie took Pop-Pop's blazer off the coat hook and put it back on.

"I can't believe Grandma thinks this is ugly," Jessie said.

"I can," Oliver said, flopping on the couch next to Hyacinth. "If we like something, Grandma is going to hate it."

"It's so weird that Mama and Grandma are related," Isa mused. "They're complete opposites."

"I think it's because Mama didn't *want* to be like her," Hyacinth said.

Jessie pulled Pop-Pop's coat around her and heard a little rustle. She stopped and patted her chest. Inside was a pocket sewn into the worn lining. Jessie slipped her fingers into the pocket and pulled out an envelope.

To Derek on his graduation day

"What's that?" Laney asked.

Isa, Oliver, and Hyacinth leaned in to get a closer look.

"It looks like a letter to Papa," Jessie said. She flipped the envelope over and saw that it was still sealed.

"Open it," Laney said.

Jessie hesitated. "It looks like Pop-Pop meant it for Papa. Maybe we should save it for him."

"Can I see it?" Laney asked.

"Just be really careful," Jessie said as she handed it over.

Laney examined the envelope and then picked at the flap closure. That minuscule gesture caused the fragile seal to break.

"I didn't think you were going to open it!" Jessie said, grabbing the envelope back.

"I didn't think it would open so easily!" Laney replied.

"I think we should read it," Oliver said. "It's already open."

"I don't know," Hyacinth said. "Maybe it's private."

"It's probably a happy graduation card," Oliver said. "Like those cards Grandma sends us every year for our birthdays with a dollar bill in them. I say we open it."

Jessie looked at Isa, and Hyacinth held her breath. Then Jessie opened the flap all the way and gently removed the folded sheets of paper inside. The ink was faded and the lines very thin, as if Pop-Pop had scratched it out with a pen that was nearly out of ink. Jessie scanned it, then cleared her throat. "I'll read it out loud."

Dear Derek,

Tomorrow I will see you graduate. I have been imagining this day since you were a young boy. When your mother was alive, we watched you learn to hold your head up for the first time and we were filled with pride. And you continued to make us proud with every little milestone: sitting up on your own, saying your first words, feeding yourself Cheerios. And all along the way, we held a dream for you close to our heart. We dreamed that you would have the opportunity to go to college. We knew it was a big dream. You would be the first one in our family to go. There were many moments when I thought it would never happen. These past two decades have been filled with so many obstacles, but you have managed to overcome each one.

Before you were born, your mom and I wanted to see the country. My father used to talk about his time at Whalers Cove when he was stationed there during the war. It sounded like a beautiful place: a shining, crystal sea; cliffs; dolphins that leaped from the waves. We had always wanted to go back there again with my dad so he could see it during peacetime. But then he passed, and your mother passed, and it was just you and me, trying to make it through the world the best we could.

A couple of years ago, I had a dream. You were in it, your mother was in it, and so was my father. We were standing on a cliff, looking out at the ocean. I could taste the salt on my lips. And I remembered my promise to go to the sea.

That dream and a long-ago promise are the

*reasons why I asked you to delay your start
day at the computer store until the end of July.
I wanted to give you the gift of this trip. I've
planned it all out. Joe says that Ludwig is
ready for us, and I've spent the last few months
working on the itinerary.*

What do you say? Are you up for a journey?

Love,

Pop-Pop

A long period of silence followed.

"Wow," Isa said. "Pop-Pop was planning a *whole trip* for Papa."

"I don't think Papa ever knew about it," Jessie said. "Pop-Pop was going to give that letter to him at graduation."

"I didn't know Papa's grandpa fought in a war," Hyacinth said.

"The Civil War?" Laney said.

Isa shook her head. "Probably World War One? Or World War Two?"

"World War Two," Jessie said. "I don't think he

would have been old enough to serve in World War I."

"Wait, there were *world* wars?" Laney asked. "Like, the whole world was in a war?"

"Yeah," Oliver said. "There were two of them."

Laney shook her head. "That's so, so terrible. And Papa's grandpa had to fight in it?"

"Well," Isa said, "it sounded like he was stationed in America. So maybe he wasn't in combat."

"Who is Joe? And who is Ludwig?" Oliver said, looking at the letter again.

"Ludwig sounds like the name of someone's owl," Hyacinth noted.

"I'm trying to think of where our great-grandfather could have been stationed," Isa said. She took out her phone and did an internet search. "That's a popular name. There are places called Whalers Cove in New York, Florida, Connecticut, Massachusetts, Arizona, California, Oregon, and Washington."

"That narrows it down," Oliver said.

While her siblings discussed the possibilities of each of those locations, Hyacinth took the letter and read it again, slowly. It made her sad that Pop-Pop never got to make that trip with Papa. It sounded like he had been working really hard on it. It sounded like a trip Papa would have loved.

Hyacinth realized that all of her siblings were staring at her.

"You have a funny look on your face," Laney said.

Hyacinth smiled. "That's because I just got the best idea."

Six

When Oliver glimpsed Hyacinth's face, he knew what she was going to say. And Oliver was already prepared *not* to like Hyacinth's idea.

"You know how we don't have a birthday present for Papa yet?" Hyacinth said.

"I thought the party was his present," Oliver said, repeating his reasoning from the morning.

"It's a big birthday," Hyacinth said, ignoring Oliver, "and I think we should do something *really* special for him. She paused. "We should take Papa on a trip to Whalers Cove for his birthday present."

Isa, Jessie, Hyacinth, and Laney all grinned, and the dark cloud that filled Oliver's chest got even heavier.

"I love it!" Isa said.

"That's brilliant," Jessie added.

"A trip to the ocean!" Laney said.

"What do you think?" Hyacinth asked, looking at Oliver hopefully. "I mean, it would mean a lot of work trying to figure out where Whalers Cove is, and—"

"I think it's a terrible idea," he interrupted.

Hyacinth's face fell.

"Why?" Jessie demanded.

"Because that letter," Oliver said, pointing to the piece of paper, "makes no sense unless we could ask Pop-Pop questions. Which we can't, obviously."

"We can't ask questions, but there are clues in this letter," Isa said reasonably.

"Like what?" Oliver said, unable to keep the words from coming out of his mouth. "Some random place called Whalers Cove? People we've never heard of, like Ludwig and Joe? Going on a trip that will most likely cost a fortune? Trying to figure this all out by *Saturday* for Papa's birthday, all while having Grandma and Grandpa around? And in case you forgot, *I* was supposed to go on a trip with Papa. And now you're thinking of a whole big trip with *everyone*?"

And because he knew he was being unreasonable

and had hurt Hyacinth's feelings, and because he missed his dad and was sad about the canceled alone time with him, and because his grandma always made him feel bad with her side comments about him, Oliver had the sudden need to disappear.

He ran up the stairs to his bedroom and slammed the door. He climbed up to his bed and pulled out a sandwich bag under his pillow with the two cookies he had saved from dessert the night before. He was about to eat one when there was a knock on the door.

Hyacinth peeked her head in. "Can I come in?"

Oliver didn't trust himself to say anything, so he kept quiet.

Hyacinth stepped tentatively into his bedroom. "I'm sorry," she said. "That was really insensitive of me to suggest a trip when your camping trip with Papa just got canceled. And my Whalers Cove idea is silly anyway. You're right: We don't have enough information about Pop-Pop or the trip. I know you're having a really bad day and you probably don't want to talk to me, but I just wanted you to know that none of us want to get in the way of your Adirondacks trip, especially me."

Hyacinth backed up and let herself out the door, closing it gently.

Oliver should have felt better, but he only felt worse. He shoved the bag of cookies back under his pillow, no longer in the mood to eat anything. He looked up at the ceiling and stared at all the stickers he had collected from various fruits over the years: pink lady apples from the United States, avocados from Mexico, mangos from the Philippines.

He started counting the stickers, something he did when he was trying to be un-mad. As it often did, the counting worked. By the time he had counted all 354 stickers, his feelings of disappointment had turned more to resignation and shame.

Then he thought about what it might mean for Papa to know that Pop-Pop had been planning a trip for them and how special it would be to take Papa to that same spot his grandfather had loved.

Hopping off his bed, Oliver headed into Jessie and Isa's room. No one was there, so he pushed aside the piles of clothes Jessie had left on her desk chair and sat down to use the computer. He searched for Whalers Cove and immediately eliminated all the areas that were not by an ocean. He then ripped a piece of blank paper out of Jessie's science notebook and made a list of the remaining locations, finding places in New York, Massachusetts, Washington State, California, Oregon, and Florida.

Oliver left his sisters' room, stopped by his to grab the bag of cookies, and made his way into Hyacinth's. She was sitting on her bed, a bunk she shared with Laney. Somehow she had managed to get Franz up on the top bunk with her.

"Hey," Oliver said.

Hyacinth looked down at him. "Hi."

Franz rested his head on the bunk railing, looking down at Oliver with his droopy eyes.

"Sorry I was such a jerk," Oliver said.

"No, I'm sorry," Hyacinth said. "I was insensitive."

"You could never be insensitive," Oliver said. "You were thinking about something nice to do for Papa. You're always trying to do nice things for people."

Hyacinth shook her head. "I got it wrong this time."

"Actually, I think it's a great idea. Look, I did some searches on Whalers Cove locations." Oliver showed her his paper. "If we do more research, I think we can find the exact spot where Papa's grandpa was stationed during the war. Maybe we could take Papa there before school starts."

Hyacinth looked at the list. "I don't know. That's a lot of states. And there's not even anyone we can ask about this. Papa's parents are gone, and he doesn't have any brothers or sisters. How will we know if we find the right place?"

Oliver smiled. "Because even though we've never met Pop-Pop, he's still our family. I think we'll know when we've found it."

Hyacinth leaned down to rest her chin on Franz's forehead. "I know what you mean. It's like how I knew Franz was going to be my dog the first time I saw him. And how Papa knew that he was going to marry Mama just by hearing her voice over the phone."

Oliver nodded. Papa loved to talk about how he fell in love with Mama when he worked in his college's tech help department and Mama called in about a computer problem. "Come on, let's talk to everyone else. If this is going to be Papa's birthday present, we have less than a week to pull it off!"

✦ ✦ ✦

Down in the basement, Isa practiced the violin, while in the living room, Aunt Penny sat on the couch checking her email and Jessie taught Laney how to blow out the inside of an egg. There were a bunch of cracked eggs on the old plastic shower curtain they'd used to cover the dining room table.

"I think we can keep the top hole little," Jessie said as she put aside yet another broken egg, "but we need to widen the bottom hole. It's too small to let the stuff go out."

While they were testing Jessie's hypothesis, Oliver and Hyacinth came downstairs.

"We have come up with a plan—" Oliver stopped in his tracks at the sight of Jessie with her mouth on the top of an egg. A trail of raw egg swung from the bottom. "What are you doing?"

Jessie raised her eyebrows but didn't stop blowing. She didn't want to lose her momentum.

"We're making the eggs hollow so we can paint them," Laney explained. "Ms. Abruzzi gave me a book with all these pictures of painted eggs because people living in Eastern Europe love to paint eggs and they call it pysanka. I want to try, and Jessie said she would help me!"

Ms. Abruzzi, the children's librarian at their local library, was always giving Laney craft ideas. For once, this activity actually interested Jessie, but more because of the science of egg blowing than the decorating.

"That's disgusting," Oliver said at the same time a huge glob of egg innards squeezed out of the bottom hole and dropped to the table.

Jessie lifted the egg triumphantly.

Laney jumped up and did an egg victory dance while Oliver and Hyacinth looked at each other in mutual confusion. Over on the couch, Aunt Penny had fallen asleep despite the commotion and was snoring lightly. A moment later, Isa came up from the basement and made a face when she saw the dining room table.

"What's going on?" she asked.

"I'm sorry to break up this weird egg thing," Oliver said, "but Hyacinth and I talked, and I'm on board with figuring out the Whalers Cove trip for Papa."

Jessie smiled. She had known that Oliver would come around.

"I did a little research," Oliver continued, handing Isa his list. "I eliminated locations that weren't by an ocean."

"Nice," Isa said, "but how are we going to find the *exact* location?"

"Why don't we split up the states?" Jessie suggested. "Oliver, you look into the locations in New York and Massachusetts; Isa, you do Washington State and Oregon; Hyacinth and Laney can do Florida; and I'll do California."

"How are we going to find information?" Laney asked.

"The internet?" Oliver suggested.

Jessie held up her phone. "I'm going to do research on this."

"We don't know how to use the internet," Laney said, pointing to herself and Hyacinth.

"It's okay," Hyacinth said. "We can go to the library."

"I can take you," Isa offered. "I've got some books to return."

"Can you return my books for me?" Oliver and Jessie said at the same time.

While Laney and Hyacinth got ready to leave, Jessie felt vaguely guilty as she brought down two huge science books that each weighed as much as Franz and put them next to a tall pile of novels that Oliver had collected.

Isa sighed when she saw the stacks of books by the door. "Are you kidding me?"

"Don't worry!" Jessie said as she brought the red Radio Flyer wagon from the basement and rolled it to the front door. "You can take the wagon."

"I want to ride in it!" Laney said.

"You know I don't like rolling that wagon to the library," Isa complained as she watched Jessie load it up with books. "Carrying it up the library steps is such a pain."

"Use the back entrance," Jessie suggested. "Where the ramps are."

"It's been under construction for the last week," Isa said. "I know that because I was just there returning your books three days ago."

By the time Hyacinth and Laney loaded their books into the wagon, it was too full for Laney to climb in. Isa, noticing that it was raining again, threw a tarp over the wagon and opened the front door.

"Where are you going?" Grandma demanded, appearing at the top of the stairs.

"Library!" Isa said, and Jessie watched her sisters rush away, the wagon bouncing behind them over the bumps and cracks of the sidewalk.

"I'm fine, by the way," Grandma said, glaring at Jessie. "Thanks for asking."

Jessie swallowed. Why hadn't *she* volunteered to go to the library? "Hey, Grandma. How are you feeling?"

"I just said I was fine," Grandma snapped as she made her way downstairs, Grandpa following her.

Aunt Penny woke up from her nap, rubbed her eyes, and asked Jessie whether it would be okay if she took a shower. Jessie gave her directions to where she could find spare towels, then turned back to her grandparents. Grandma was staring at the dining room table in horror. Jessie had forgotten about the eggs.

"I was helping Laney with an art project," Jessie explained. Grandma did not seem impressed.

While Jessie cleaned, Oliver went to the kitchen and helped himself to a cookie from the Tupperware Mama had left on the counter.

"Oliver!" Grandma chastised.

"Oh, sorry," Oliver said, his mouth full of cookie. He offered the container to Grandma. "Do you want one?"

"You eat way too many sweets," Grandma said. "It's not good for you."

Oliver shrugged. "Mama says that as long as we eat a balanced diet and get exercise, a couple of cookies a day isn't a big deal."

Grandpa walked over and selected a cookie. He took a bite and smiled.

Grandma sniffed. "Do you have real food?"

"There's some leftovers in the refrigerator," Jessie said. "I'll reheat them for you after I'm done cleaning. Grandpa, are you hungry?" Neither of her grandparents had eaten much at lunch.

Grandpa nodded.

After the dining table was cleared, Jessie pulled leftovers from last night's dinner out of the refrigerator, split the noodles and broth into two bowls, and stuck them in the microwave. At the same time, she kept an ear on Grandma's conversation with Oliver.

"How are your grades?" Grandma asked Oliver.

"They're okay," Oliver said. "I mean, not as good as Jessie's, but I'm passing all of my classes."

Grandma's eyes narrowed.

"Oliver has been training with the high school basketball team," Jessie chimed in from the kitchen. "He's getting really good."

"Basketball?" Grandma asked in a tone one would generally reserve for "pinkeye."

"Yep," Jessie said. "If he keeps it up, he'll go right to the varsity team as a freshman. That's pretty much unheard of."

Oliver beamed, but Jessie noticed that Grandma wasn't impressed by basketball. So Jessie added, "Oliver is a great English student. Much better than me. He reads all the time."

Grandma didn't respond, which made Jessie think that neither basketball nor English thrilled her. But Oliver didn't seem bothered by Grandma's disapproval. He had wandered over to the couch and was now reading. Grandpa was next to him, trying to keep Franz from snatching his third cookie.

Jessie took the bowls from the microwave and set them on the table with napkins and chopsticks. Grandpa sat down and started eating right away, but Grandma sniffed the noodles suspiciously, as if she thought Jessie had sneaked poison into her bowl when she wasn't looking. Jessie rolled her eyes and went to the kitchen to clean up. When she was done washing the stacks of dishes left in the sink from the morning, she turned around to see Grandma finishing her last bite of noodles. Grandpa was already done and was helping himself to another cookie.

"Good?" Jessie asked Grandma, taking the empty bowls to wash.

Grandma wiped her mouth with a napkin. She didn't say anything, but she did nod, which Jessie thought was better than nothing.

It was weird, Jessie thought as she washed the rest of the dishes, that she had nothing to say to the grandparents who were in their home at that very moment. She would give anything to sit down with Pop-Pop and ask him questions. When she was done cleaning, she dried her hands and turned around. Her grandparents were gone, presumably back upstairs to Mama and Papa's room.

So Jessie took out her phone, sat at the dining room table, and started to research all the Whalers Coves in California, hoping she could learn more about the family she had never known.

Seven

Hyacinth watched as Isa grunted and lugged the unwieldy wagon up the stairs to the library. Rainwater that had pooled on the tarp splashed onto her pants and shoes. Laney tried to help but only made the wagon tilt precariously and threaten to dump their books. When Isa finally got the wagon up to the entrance, she rested.

"I hope I didn't strain an arm muscle," she grumbled. "Mr. Van Hooten will kill me."

Mr. Van Hooten was Isa's violin teacher, and he had prohibited Isa from doing anything that might injure her fingers or arms. That was why she never played basketball, volleyball, or softball. Once, a few years ago, she had played basketball during PE and sprained two fingers. Mr. Van Hooten had marched to her school and had words with the gym instructors. After that, Isa ran laps whenever they played sports with high finger-injury possibilities.

Hyacinth loved the library. Walking through those heavy wooden doors and breathing in the smell of books always gave her a feeling of possibility, as if the whole world were waiting for her to discover it. Isa pulled the wagon to the check-in counter, and together the three sisters started unloading books.

"Hey there, Vanderbeekers!" Ms. Abruzzi said. As usual, she was wearing an outfit that Hyacinth adored: a silk blouse printed with cats wearing reading glasses, a chunky necklace of large yellow beads, and big glasses with leopard-print frames.

"We've got books to return," Isa said, heaving up one of the science books. "Again."

"I see you needed the wagon today," Ms. Abruzzi said, peeking over her big wooden desk.

"Jessie and Oliver wanted us to bring in their books," Laney informed her.

"Can we leave the wagon here while we look around?" Isa asked Ms. Abruzzi.

"Of course. Just park it over there in the corner."

Isa pulled the wagon to the corner while Hyacinth stayed by the circulation desk.

"Anything I can help you with, Hyacinth?" Ms. Abruzzi asked.

"We're trying to find out where my great-grandfather was stationed during World War Two," Hyacinth told her.

"That sounds like a great project. Is this for school?"

"No. We found an old letter that said our great-grandfather fought in a war and was stationed somewhere called Whalers Cove, but that's all we know about him. We think World War Two makes the most sense."

Isa had rejoined them by then, and she stood by, waiting to hear what Ms. Abruzzi would say.

"Hmm . . ." Ms. Abruzzi tapped her pen against her chin. "That's not much to go on. I think the National Personnel Records Center needs certain information, but let me check." She turned to her computer and typed rapidly. "Yes, you would need the complete name as used in service, the service number, the branch of service, date and place of birth, and dates of service."

Isa shook her head. "We only have his name and not any of that other information."

"What are you trying to find out, exactly?" Ms. Abruzzi asked.

Hyacinth told Ms. Abruzzi about the letter and their plans to re-create Pop-Pop's trip.

"Ah," Ms. Abruzzi said. "Let's see if we can at least find out if Whalers Cove shows up in any of the World War Two books."

Ms. Abruzzi stood and the Vanderbeekers followed her. Hyacinth noticed that her favorite librarian's outfit was even more awesome now that she could see the whole thing. Ms. Abruzzi wore silver pants and black-and-white zebra-patterned boots. Hyacinth wondered if she could make shoes like that by painting white stripes on her black boots.

With the efficiency of a woman who had worked in that very library building for two decades, Ms. Abruzzi marched over to a stack, scanned it briefly, and plucked three huge books from the shelves. She brought them to an empty wooden table, took the top one off the pile, and flipped to the index. Isa did the same with a second book, and Hyacinth did the same with the last.

"What are you looking for?" Laney asked.

"I'm just doing a quick search for Whalers Cove to see if anything comes up," Ms. Abruzzi said. "Nope, not in this book."

"Not in this one either," Isa said, closing the book.

"Or here," Hyacinth said.

"I could check the other libraries to see if they have any books about World War Two sites in North America," Ms. Abruzzi suggested, gathering the books to reshelve.

"I want to check those out," Laney said, nodding at the books in Ms. Abruzzi's arms.

"Really?" Isa and Hyacinth said.

"I want to learn more about the war," Laney said.

"These books are going to be really hard to read," Isa told her. "Maybe Ms. Abruzzi can suggest some that would be easier."

"Yes, we can go upstairs to the children's department—" Ms. Abruzzi began, but Laney interrupted her.

"I want these," Laney said. She grabbed the book on top of the stack that Ms. Abruzzi was holding, staggering once the weight of the volume was fully in her arms.

Hyacinth reached down to help, but Laney shook her head and stumbled to the circulation desk. Ms. Abruzzi brought the other two books to the desk and put them on the counter, then scanned Isa's library card. After she processed the three World War II books, she pulled out a stack of books she had set aside for Oliver. They were an eclectic mix of books in verse, contemporary realistic fiction, fantasy, and historical fiction.

"Should I go ahead and put these on your card?" Ms. Abruzzi asked Isa.

Isa sighed and nodded. Hyacinth stealthily added a pile of craft and recipe books to the stack.

"And that brings you up to forty-nine checkouts," Ms. Abruzzi said to Isa.

"I'm glad we brought the wagon today," Isa told her.

The Vanderbeekers waved goodbye to their favorite librarian, loaded up the wagon, and headed back down the stairs. It was still raining, big drops splashing on the sidewalk.

"Oof, this is even heavier than it was before," Isa said. "I thought we were only picking up a few books."

Hyacinth and Laney looked at their big sister.

"I feel like you don't know us at all," Hyacinth said.

"Can we stop by Castleman's Bakery on the way home?" Laney asked. "Please? Pretty please?"

"I feel like you don't know *me* at all," Isa said, veering toward Castleman's, their trusty red wagon bumping down the sidewalk behind them.

✧ ✧ ✧

There were many places that felt like home to the Vanderbeekers: the brownstone, of course, but also Mama's cat café, the library, the community garden, and Castleman's Bakery. In fact, one of Laney's first memories was going to Castleman's Bakery with Papa on Saturday mornings. Mrs. Castleman would always give her a star cookie as big as her hand, and Mr. Castleman would emerge from the back kitchen with a piece of dough for her to play with. Laney loved the way it squished in her hands.

The bakery was busy, with customers placing large orders of flaky cheese croissants and sweet apple turnovers. While Isa parked their wagon in an empty nook under the side counter, where the sugar packets, coffee stirrers, and milk were kept, Hyacinth and Laney got in line. The bakery, protected from rain, was a welcome respite.

While they waited, Laney examined the framed newspaper articles written about the bakery hanging along the wall.

"A Cozy Home Bakery in Harlem," said one headline.

"The Castlemans Give Croissants the Royal Treatment," said another.

Laney peered closer at the articles and realized that they were yellowed with age. That reminded her that Mr. and Mrs. Castleman had been around for a long time.

A few minutes later, the Vanderbeekers got to the front of the line. Mrs. Castleman smiled when she saw them.

"Hello, my friends. What can I get you today?" Mrs. Castleman asked.

"We are in desperate need of chocolate croissants," Isa said.

Mrs. Castleman took a piece of wax paper from the dispenser and began putting chocolate croissants into a bag.

Laney looked through the display case at Mrs. Castleman's hand reaching for the pastries.

"Mrs. Castleman, did you ever know Papa's dad?" Laney asked.

Mrs. Castleman's face broke into a big smile. "Of course I knew him. Pop-Pop came in here almost every morning for a cup of coffee. One sugar, heavy on the milk."

"Really?" Laney said.

Mrs. Castleman nodded. "He started coming in when we first opened. Your father was around ten years old, and they would come here after Pop-Pop was done coaching the basketball league at the Y. Your dad used to play in that league."

"Really?" said Isa, surprised.

"Oh yes," Mrs. Castleman said. "That was a big thing they shared. Didn't your dad teach Oliver how to play?"

"I guess he did," Isa said. "Him and Uncle Arthur."

Mrs. Castleman nodded. "Pop-Pop would bring in your dad and all the kids in the league and buy them whatever they wanted. I always sold a lot of croissants when they came by. I gave them extra when I could. Pop-Pop couldn't have made much money driving garbage trucks around."

"He drove garbage trucks?" Isa said.

"Just like Mr. Mark?" Laney asked.

"Just like Mr. Mark," Mrs. Castleman said.

"I guess I never asked what he did for a living,"

Isa said.

"Did Pop-Pop ever mention anything about Whalers Cove?" Hyacinth asked.

Mrs. Castleman squinted, thinking. "No, I don't remember him ever saying anything about a Whalers Cove."

Isa's phone chirped, and Laney peeked at the screen and saw that it was Benny.

"Benny's shift starts in an hour, and he wants to know if I can hang out with him for half an hour before," Isa told Hyacinth and Laney.

"You should do it," Hyacinth said. "We can walk home by ourselves."

"Nice try," Isa said, knowing how much Hyacinth and Laney wanted to have more independence, "but I'll walk you home first."

"I want to read my books and do research on Whalers Cove," Laney said.

"Don't worry about us," Hyacinth said.

Isa nodded, and Laney helped Isa gather the wagon, maneuver it out of the bakery, and head for 141st Street. On their way home, Isa's phone chirped again.

"Benny again?" Hyacinth asked.

Isa shook her head. "It's Papa. He got to Indiana safe, but his flight was very turbulent."

"What does that mean?" Laney asked. Except for Jessie, none of the Vanderbeeker siblings had ever been on a plane.

"It means it was really bumpy."

"That sounds scary," Hyacinth said.

"I want to talk to him," Laney said. "Can he call now?"

"He said he would call tonight," Isa said, putting the phone in her pocket.

As she munched on her pastry, Laney absorbed the new information she had learned about her grandfather. It made her even more curious about her dad's family, and stories about Pop-Pop were definitely on her list of things to talk to him about when he called later.

Eight

Oliver sat in his bedroom. He had been researching Whalers Cove on Jessie's computer when Grandma emerged from Mama's bedroom and asked why he was spending so much time online. Then she told him he should do homework, and when he explained that he didn't have any homework during the summer, she looked completely horrified.

To get away from her, he headed to the backyard. On his way through the kitchen, he noticed Grandpa at the sink dismantling the faucet handle.

"What are you doing?" Oliver asked.

"It leaks," Grandpa said as he inspected the parts inside the faucet.

Oliver, hearing Grandma coming down the stairs,

slipped out the door. He knew Grandma wasn't a fan of chickens, so he would be safe outside. Climbing up to his treehouse, he hid himself among the thousands of leaves and got some protection from the rain. A knot of sparrows had the same idea—they were right above him, chattering wildly.

The gate at the side of the building gave a squeak, and Oliver looked down to see Mr. Beiderman entering the backyard. He headed straight to the tree and began climbing the ladder. Oliver was stunned. Mr. Beiderman had never been in his treehouse before.

"I know I'm going to break my neck climbing this," Mr. Beiderman grumbled as he heaved himself up into the treehouse. His face was slightly red. "So, Oliver, how are things?"

"Uh, fine? What are you doing up here?"

"I heard that you're having a not-so-great day," Mr. Beiderman said. "And I know your dad went to Indiana and your mom is working, and I saw you out here alone and thought I'd see how you were."

Oliver stared through the trees. He could see Jimmy L's apartment across the way, and he wished his friend were home and not a thousand miles away.

"It hasn't been the best," Oliver admitted.

Mr. Beiderman nodded in understanding.

They sat in silence for a while, listening to the chickens clucking away below them and the city sounds—ambulance sirens, cooing pigeons, and the steady beat of music coming from a stereo.

"I'm sorry to hear about your canceled camping trip," Mr. Beiderman said. "When does your dad get back from Indiana?"

"Thursday," Oliver said. "And Grandma and Grandpa are probably going to stay all week."

"I'm sorry," Mr. Beiderman said. "Would it help if Orlando and I came over for dinner tonight? It might provide a distraction, right? I'll order pizza for us."

Oliver shook his head. "Well, Grandma is going to think that's too unhealthy."

Mr. Beiderman shrugged. "Too bad. Now can we get down from here? I'm hungry and need a cookie ASAP."

❖ ❖ ❖

As they made their way back inside, Oliver told Mr. Beiderman about the new hair place that had just opened up on Frederick Douglass Boulevard. A lot of kids in Oliver's school had gone in there with regular hair and come out with awesome hair. Their boring brown or black or blond or red hair was now all the colors of the rainbow. The other day, Oliver had seen a guy emerge from the salon with bright green spiky hair.

Aunt Penny, who was sitting at the dining room table learning how to knit with Hyacinth and Laney, looked up at their entrance and overheard their conversation.

"Trust me, you do *not* want to do that to your hair," Aunt Penny interjected.

"Why not?" Oliver said.

Aunt Penny held up her knitting, observed all the holes in her project, then showed it to Hyacinth, who looked at it and shook her head sadly.

"You have to start over," Hyacinth told her.

As Aunt Penny removed the stitches from the needle and started winding the yarn back into the ball, she said, "I've never dyed my hair, but that's probably because I saw what happened to Uncle Arthur."

"Uncle Arthur dyed his hair?" Oliver asked.

"And had it shaved around the bottom. That was back when he was in high school."

"Cool!" Oliver and Laney said.

"I have a photo!" Aunt Penny said, and pulled out her phone. She opened up the offending photo. "I made it his profile picture. It bugs him so much."

"Whoa," Oliver said, looking at a much younger Uncle Arthur sporting pink hair that was long on top and shaved at the bottom. The longer hairs were combed to the side and hung over his left eye. "That looks so awesome."

"He tried to use food coloring first, but his hair was so dark it didn't work. So he saved up money from mowing lawns and got it done at a hair salon. Only he didn't make that much money mowing lawns, so he went to a place where you could pay less if you were willing to have a stylist-in-training do your hair. And since she was just learning, she didn't really know how to bleach his super-dark hair."

"What happened?" Laney asked.

"He wanted purple hair, but the stylist accidentally turned it bright pink," Aunt Penny said. "Your grandparents were horrified, especially because there was a big family gathering the next day. *Everyone* was talking about Arthur's hair."

Oliver considered Aunt Penny's story. "I still want green hair."

"Even after hearing that?" Aunt Penny said.

"Yes!"

"Your uncle Arthur had so many hair misadventures," Aunt Penny continued. "One time, he had a haircut where the back of his hair was so short that he asked the hairdresser to buzz his name in the back. Only the stylist misheard his name and wrote 'Arnold' instead."

Hyacinth, Laney, and even Mr. Beiderman started laughing, and then they had to call Uncle Arthur and make fun of him. Oliver, however, did not laugh. He was thinking. Getting his name buzzed in the back of his hair would definitely give people something to talk about on the basketball court.

Oliver hadn't known that food coloring could color hair, and now he wanted to see if it would work. Not on his own hair, since it was dark like Uncle Arthur's, but maybe on lighter-colored hair. And there was really only one living thing in the brownstone who might be a good candidate for experimentation.

Tuxedo.

Tuxedo was a black-and-white cat, and her hair was perfect for hair-dye trials. Maybe Tuxedo would look so fantastic that Mama would let Oliver dye his own hair.

Oliver figured that Laney would be on board with dying her cat's hair green. He waited until Aunt Penny and Mr. Beiderman were distracted with a conversation about famous art heists before broaching the idea with his sister.

"Sure," said Laney. "Maybe Jessie and Hyacinth will want to help."

"Ah, I think it might be better if we *surprise* them," Oliver said. He wasn't sure if Jessie or Hyacinth would love this plan.

"Okay," Laney said happily. She loved surprises.

Mama didn't use food coloring very much, but they found some old tubes deep in the back of the cupboard behind the muffin and popover pans. The box had only two out of four tubes left, and Oliver was happy to see that green and red were the two choices.

"How much do you think we'll need?" Oliver asked Laney.

"All of it?" she suggested.

Laney trotted off to find Tuxedo while Oliver went into the bathroom and twisted the cap off the food coloring. A few minutes later, Laney returned with Tuxedo in her arms. She was drowsy from being woken up from her late-afternoon nap and was purring contentedly.

"How should we do this?" Oliver asked. "Just squirt it on her fur and rub it in?"

"Sure," Laney said. "You can use my comb if you want."

So Oliver squirted some dots on Tuxedo's fur and rubbed it in with his hands while Laney combed the dye through. After a few more drops, Oliver took a critical look at Tuxedo. The cat loved being groomed and didn't seem bothered about being green.

"I think we should use a lot more," Oliver said. "I want her to look like a shamrock."

Laney shrugged. "If you say so."

Oliver took the tube and squeezed it hard, and a whole lot of food coloring squirted out, splattering the bath mat in the process.

"Whoa," Laney said.

Tuxedo took that opportunity to shake her whole

body as if she were a wet dog, causing green food coloring to spray all over the bathroom, the white towels hanging by the door, and Oliver and Laney.

Laney pointed at Oliver. "You have green splotches all over your face now!"

Oliver didn't want to stand up and look in the mirror—that would require him to let go of Tuxedo—so they continued to comb food coloring into Tuxedo's hair until her white fur was a very pleasing emerald green color.

"She looks amazing," Oliver said. This could totally convince Mama that he should be allowed to dye his hair.

"I want to dye my hair too," Laney said. She picked up the red food coloring and held it out to her brother. "Can we try with this?"

"Sure," Oliver said. He took the top off, and seeing how much food coloring it took to get Tuxedo's hair green, he went ahead and squirted the whole bottle over Laney's head.

"Oliver!" Laney squealed. "It's dripping!"

Oliver handed her a washcloth, and she wiped her face.

"Oops," Laney said when she saw the red stains all over the washcloth.

"It'll wash out," Oliver said as he combed. This time, he didn't rub the dye in, not wanting to ruin the effect of his green hands. Because of that, the red dye was getting everywhere—it was dripping on his clothes, on Laney's clothes, and on the tile floor.

"Is it working?" Laney asked.

"I'm not sure," Oliver said. "Maybe."

When he was done combing it in, Oliver was pretty sure that Laney's hair had a nice red tint to it.

Laney pulled out the step stool so she could get a look in the mirror.

"Oh no, my face!"

Oliver looked at his sister's reflection in the mirror. Her face was all blotchy and red from the dye that had dripped down after the initial squeeze.

"It'll wash out," Oliver said again, and he watched as Laney scrubbed her face until it turned all pink and rosy. The red dye remained.

"I wouldn't worry about it," Oliver told her, then thought about Uncle Arthur buzzing his name in the back of his hair. "Want to help me shave Franz's hair?"

The sound of the doorbell ringing disrupted the relative quiet of the brownstone.

"Pizza's here!" Jessie called from her bedroom, and Oliver and Laney opened the bathroom door and raced toward the front door. Franz beat them there, and Tuxedo was close behind.

Oliver peeked out the window. It was Austin, one of the guys who delivered pizza from Famous Original Ray's Pizza on 139th Street and Lenox Avenue. Ray's Original made the best New York City pizza: enough cheese to satisfy even cheese-loving Laney, perfect red sauce, and a thin, crispy crust.

Oliver opened the door. "Hi, Austin."

Austin looked up from the order slip taped onto the pizza. "Whoa, what happened to you?"

"Food dye!" Laney said.

"And your parents are okay with that?"

"Our parents aren't here," Laney told him.

Austin got a glimpse of green Tuxedo. "Oh my gosh, your poor cat."

"I think Tuxedo looks great," Oliver said. "I'm hoping it will convince my mom to let me dye my hair green."

Austin broke into a big grin. "Good luck with that!"

"Money is on the side table!" Mr. Beiderman called from the kitchen. "Keep the change."

Laney took the pizza while Oliver gave Austin the money and said goodbye.

"Thanks for getting the pizza," Jessie said to Mr. Beiderman as she came down the stairs. Laney was on her way to the dining room to set down the hot pizza when Tuxedo dashed across the living room and Jessie screamed.

"What happened to Tuxedo?" she screeched.

Laney, startled by Jessie's outburst, dropped the pizza box, which tipped just enough for the lid to flip open, and the pizza landed face-down on the ground. By that time, Jessie had made it all the way down the stairs and was now looking at horror at Laney and Oliver.

"What happened to your faces? And your hands?"

Laney, knowing she was in big trouble, raced past Jessie and, in a moment of panicked folly, stuck her head between the spindles halfway up the stairs. She was so distressed, however, that she pushed extra hard and her head popped through, something that had never happened before.

"Help!" Laney said. "I'm stuck!"

"Just pull your head out," Jessie said. "If you got it in there, you can get it out."

"It hurts!" Laney said as she attempted to pull her head back out. "I'm going to be stuck here forever!"

Mr. Beiderman and Aunt Penny raced to the stairs.

"Maybe we can rub her whole head with oil or butter," Aunt Penny said.

"No!" Laney said. She started crying.

"It will help you slide out," Mr. Beiderman told her.

"No!"

"Don't touch her! I'll get her free!" Oliver declared, and he ran down to the basement, where Mr. Smiley's saw was stored under the staircase from when Papa had borrowed it the previous week. By the time he returned, both Grandma and Grandpa were awake and trying to pull Laney free while she screamed, Franz was barking up a storm, Tuxedo had gotten the zoomies and was racing back and forth through the living room, and Jessie was scolding everyone from the foot of the stairs.

"Don't worry," Oliver said, almost beheading Jessie as he held the saw aloft. "I've got this." He ran up the stairs and prepared to saw the spindles and grant his sister her freedom.

"I don't know if this is such a great idea," Mr. Beiderman said, looking very uncomfortable.

"I don't want to be stuck here forever!" Laney cried, tears dripping down her face.

As Mr. Beiderman approached the stairs, Oliver got the saw ready, afraid Mr. B would take away the tool before he could free his sister.

"Don't worry, Laney," Oliver said. "I've got this all under control."

Nine

The rain had stopped by the time Isa headed back to the bakery. The sun glistened off wet windowpanes and slick streets. Cars and trucks flooded the avenues with their squeaky brakes and rumbling engines, and when Isa got to Castleman's, the windows were so fogged up from the humid weather that she couldn't see inside. She opened the door and found that the afternoon rush had subsided. Benny was sitting at a table and snacking on an apple turnover. He smiled when he saw her.

"Hey," Benny said. "You want anything to eat?"

Isa shook her head. "I just had a chocolate croissant, but thanks."

Benny had only half an hour to chat before his

shift, so he told her about the new workout regimen his basketball coach had them doing. Isa, who did not consider herself athletic at all, listened patiently as he talked about interval training. Then she told Benny about her dad leaving and her grandparents arriving in town. By then, it was four o'clock and time for Benny's shift.

Isa was saying goodbye when Mrs. Castleman emerged from the kitchen, her apron off and her jacket on.

"I am done for the day," Mrs. Castleman said to Benny, then turned to Isa. "If you have time, can you walk me home? I've been thinking about your grandfather since Laney mentioned him, and I wanted to tell you a story."

Isa didn't have to think twice. She nodded and followed Mrs. Castleman out the door, and they headed north toward the Castlemans' apartment.

"One thing I remembered about your grandfather," Mrs. Castleman began, "is that he loved birds. He would collect bird books so he could learn to identify them. He was always sharing some piece of information he had learned about a bird with me, even though he knew I wasn't such a fan. I found birds a nuisance, especially pigeons. I couldn't stand those birds! Then, one summer evening, Pop-Pop came into the bakery right before we closed. I think your dad was around twelve. Your grandfather was so excited because there was a really rare bird in Central Park and he wanted me to see it. So he forced Mr. Castleman and me to close the bakery a few minutes early and we walked down to the Harlem Meer. And there, floating in the lake among the mallards, was the strangest duck I had ever seen. It had a bright red beak, a strip of emerald green feathers on the top of its head, a purple chest, and black and white stripes around its neck. Your dad named it Firequacker for its colorful feathers. Pop-Pop scoured his bird books to identify it, and it turned out to be a Mandarin duck. They're native to China and Japan, and no one knew how one had ended up in Central Park! The duck stayed for about a week, and your dad would come by the bakery every evening to pick us up and take us to the Harlem Meer to see the bird. Then it flew off and we never saw it again."

"Wow," Isa said. "I had no idea he loved birds so much."

"The great thing about your grandfather," Mrs. Castleman said, "was that he wanted to share his joy with everyone he knew. It didn't matter that I didn't find birds fascinating. He taught me to appreciate them. Even pigeons! I've been trying to go down to the park once a week to feed the birds since Pop-Pop died."

They had reached Mrs. Castleman's building by then.

"And that small action reminds me to find beauty in the world," she told Isa. "Do you have a few minutes? I want to show you something."

Isa nodded and followed Mrs. Castleman inside, and they got into the elevator and went up to the eleventh floor. The elevator doors separated and Mrs. Castleman led the way to apartment 11F. She opened the door, and Isa smiled. Entering the Castlemans' home was like stepping into a forest. Hanging from hooks bolted into the ceiling were lush green plants with long trailing vines. Miniature trees thrived in big round planters on the floor. Pots in a rainbow of colors sat

on windowsills, leaves as big as Isa's head fanning out from their stems.

Mrs. Castleman went to a bookshelf in her living room and pulled down a box. Inside were stacks of photographs, and Isa looked with interest as she saw younger versions of the Castlemans standing in front of their bakery. The storefront looked different back then, with a dark green awning of scalloped edges with blocky white letters instead of the hand-painted wooden sign that hung there now.

Mrs. Castleman found the picture she was looking for and handed it to Isa. The photo showed the Castlemans, a boy, and man standing by a lake. Off in the background was a flock of ducks.

Mrs. Castleman pointed to the boy. "That's your dad," she said. Then she pointed to the tall man, who had a smile that filled his face. "That is your grandfather." Then she pointed to a tiny speck at the middle of the lake. "And that is Firequacker."

Isa squinted at the photo. She could not tell the difference between Firequacker and all the other ducks, but the fact that they had taken a photo must have meant that it was an important bird. More interesting to Isa were the images of her dad and Pop-Pop. Now that she thought about it, she had not seen many photos of them. In the brownstone, there were many framed photos of her and her siblings at various ages, but just one of Pop-Pop with Papa. It made her wonder if Papa had a scrapbook of old photos he could share with her.

She must have been looking at the photo for a very long time, because she started when she felt Mrs. Castleman put a hand on her shoulder. "You can keep that photo, if you want."

Isa looked up. "Really?"

"Yes, of course," Mrs. Castleman said. "Here's one more."

Isa took another photo from her, this one of Pop-Pop alongside a teenager wearing a basketball jersey.

"That's Jamal," Mrs. Castleman said. "One of the

kids Pop-Pop coached."

Isa had never heard about Jamal and something about the photo made her want to know everything about him.

"Actually," Isa said, pulling out her phone, "can I record you telling his story so I can replay it for my family?"

When Mrs. Castleman nodded, Isa turned on the voice recorder feature on her phone. Mrs. Castleman's words filled the air. When she was done speaking, Isa found herself holding the two photos of Pop-Pop to her heart.

"Family history is important," Mrs. Castleman said. "It's good to know where we came from. You, my dear, have a beautiful legacy."

Isa thanked Mrs. Castleman for the photos and the stories, then headed home.

Isa had never thought about her grandfather walking these streets, but given all the new information from the day—first the jacket, then the letter, and now the photos—Isa felt as if Harlem had taken on a more magical feeling. Harlem had been Pop-Pop's home like it was now hers.

She was so immersed in thinking about Pop-Pop that when she opened the door to the brownstone, the noise and chaos inside made her jump.

"Help me, Isa!" Laney yelled from the staircase.

Isa glanced over, then blinked. Laney's head was stuck between the spindles of the staircase, and Oliver was standing over her, a saw raised in his green hands.

"Oliver, freeze!" Isa yelled.

Oliver froze.

"Now come down the stairs *carefully* and hand me that saw," Isa told him.

"We told him it was a bad idea," Aunt Penny said. "We tried to call you, but there was no answer."

"Where on earth did you find this?" Isa asked after Oliver slowly made his way down the stairs and relinquished the saw.

"Papa borrowed it from Mr. Smiley, and since Mr. Smiley has been out of town, he hasn't returned it yet," Oliver said.

"Are you kidding me?" Isa asked.

"Help!" Laney called.

Isa took in the chaos around the living room, which included Franz howling with the volume of five thousand trumpets as Jessie held him by the leash.

"What's wrong with him?" Isa asked.

"Laney dropped a whole pizza on the ground before she got stuck in the stairs," Jessie said, pulling on his collar but losing the battle. "Now Franz wants the pizza."

Hyacinth was putting the pizza back into the box. "I'm cleaning it up! Don't worry!"

On closer look, Isa realized there was a long smear of red pizza sauce leading from the carpet under the couch.

Jessie, reading her sister's mind, spoke up. "Tuxedo got a piece. She dragged a whole slice under the couch. No one is small enough to grab her except Laney, but Laney is stuck."

Isa shook her head. "I wasn't gone *that* long!"

"Ninety-three minutes!" Jessie said as Franz lunged again for the pizza. "It only takes ten seconds for things to get nuts around here. You owe me."

"I've got all the pizza back in the box!" Hyacinth said. "Except that one piece under the couch. I can't reach that."

Isa looked at Mr. Beiderman and Aunt Penny.

"How could you let this happen?"

"We were talking," Aunt Penny explained, pointing to Mr. Beiderman. "He was telling me about how the *Mona Lisa* was stolen back in 1911. It was taken right off the wall at the Louvre . . ." Aunt Penny trailed off.

Isa sought out Grandma and Grandpa, but they just shrugged, innocent bystanders in this chaotic world.

"Can you get me out of here?" Laney said.

Isa then noticed Laney's face was as red as Oliver's hands were green.

"What happened to your hands?" she asked Oliver. "And your face?" she asked Laney.

"He dyed Tuxedo's hair green and my hair red!" Laney said from the stairs.

There was a pause.

"What did you say?" Isa asked.

"It wasn't my fault," Oliver said. He pointed a green finger at Aunt Penny. "It was hers."

Ten

All eyes turned toward Aunt Penny, and Hyacinth saw her aunt's face turn scarlet.

"*My* fault?" Aunt Penny said, hands up in an *I'm innocent!* gesture. "I simply showed them a picture of Uncle Arthur when he dyed his hair back in high school. I specifically used it as an example for why you *shouldn't* dye your hair!"

Isa looked as if she was about to reply, but then Laney whimpered.

"Are you sure you can't get your head out?" Isa asked, kneeling on the step next to her sister. "I mean, you got it in there, right? You must be able to get it out again."

Jessie spoke up. "My unscientific explanation is

that she stuck her head in at a very particular angle that matched perfectly with the curves of the spindles, and along with the force of her panic, that created a perfect storm of being able to pop her head through. Based on a quick visual examination, for her to replicate that situation to get her head back out would be quite difficult."

"We tried to pull her out, but she kept screaming," Grandma added.

"And she won't let us grease her head," Aunt Penny said, "although I think that would help."

"No!" Laney screeched, and Grandma put her hands to her ears.

"What a mess," Isa said.

"I'm ready to saw her out," Oliver said, reaching out to get the saw back from Isa.

Isa looked at Laney; then she nodded at Oliver. "Okay, fine. But be very careful! The last thing we need is to go to the emergency room again."

Isa handed over the saw and Oliver got down to business. The spindles were curved in a decorative way, so Oliver wisely pointed the sharp parts of the blade away from Laney and selected a section where the wood was at its narrowest point. Isa kept a protective hand on Laney's head.

A few minutes later, Oliver broke through the wood. He snapped the broken spindle away from his sister's head, and Laney was free!

"Hooray!" cheered everyone.

Laney shook her head, and sawdust flew everywhere.

"Thank you, Oliver!" she said, turning to hug him.

"Oh jeez," Isa said when she got a good look at the two of them together, speckled in red and green. "What exactly did you do?"

While Isa listened to the whole story, Hyacinth managed to use the handle of a broom to get the pizza out from under the couch. Tuxedo pounced on the broom bristles, her now-green paws also red from tomato sauce.

"I had no idea cats like pizza," Aunt Penny said as Hyacinth picked up the half-eaten piece and walked to the kitchen to throw it away.

"Tuxedo loves everything," Hyacinth told her. "She ate the whole middle out of my birthday cake back in February, and Mama had to make a new one."

Grandma looked as if she wanted to say something, but then she shook her head and went up the stairs, carefully avoiding the broken spindle, which now hung crooked from its spot. A few moments later, Hyacinth heard her parents' door close.

"Is Grandma mad at us?" Hyacinth asked.

"She's probably tired from the travel," Aunt Penny said as she watched Tuxedo groom her tomato-stained paws at Laney's feet. "Is it always like this here?"

"Yes," Oliver, Jessie, and Isa said at the same time Laney and Hyacinth said, "No."

"I'm hungry," said Grandpa, picking up a piece of pizza from the box on the table.

"Uh, Grandpa?" Hyacinth said. "You might not want to eat that. It fell on the ground."

Grandpa shrugged and took a bite anyway.

Hyacinth cringed. The floor could be extremely dirty, between their four pets and family of seven. But he seemed content eating the pizza, and everyone watched him without saying a word.

"Should I order more?" Aunt Penny said, breaking the silence.

But Mr. Beiderman was already calling the pizza place, and the Vanderbeekers got busy cleaning everything up before their mom got home.

☼ ☼ ☼

Hyacinth did her best to clean the pizza sauce from the living room carpet, but it definitely left a red stain. Mama had called; she was having trouble with one of the ovens and had to wait for a repair person to come, so she would not be home for dinner. It gave the Vanderbeekers more time to clean, which was good because the bathroom was a mess too. Jessie and Isa spent twenty minutes scrubbing the dye-stained towels before giving up and stuffing them into the washing machine, along with a whole lot of detergent, and hoping for the best. By the time the apartment had been cleaned to the best of their ability, Grandma had come back downstairs and two more pizzas had arrived, along with Miss Josie and Orlando.

"Hello, hello!" Miss Josie said, then looked closer at Oliver and Laney. "What happened to you?"

"A food dye experiment gone wrong," Oliver said.

Miss Josie nodded as if this was completely normal. "And how is your father doing?"

"He got to Indiana safely," Jessie said. "We were glad because it was so stormy this morning. Orlando, where've you been today? You missed a heroic rescue by Oliver."

"He sawed through the staircase railing when my head got stuck in the spindles," Laney told them.

Oliver bowed. "I accept tips in cash or cookies."

"Wow," Orlando said. "I'm really sorry I missed that."

"I was amazing," Oliver told him.

"How about dinner?" Mr. Beiderman interjected. "Set the table, will you?"

Oliver headed to the kitchen to grab napkins and plates, and Aunt Penny brought the new pizza pies to the dining room table.

While Hyacinth fed Franz, her family and their guests took their seats. As a result, by the time she was finished, she was stuck with the last choice of chairs: the one empty spot was between Grandpa and Aunt Penny. She didn't mind Aunt Penny, but Grandpa scared her. She considered asking Oliver, who had gotten a seat between Orlando and Miss Josie, if he would switch with her, but it was so loud she'd have to shout, and she didn't want to risk having anybody hear the reason she didn't want to sit next to Grandpa.

People were already biting into slices of hot, thin-crust pizza before she even sat down. The seats were crammed so close together that Hyacinth had to pull the chair all the way out before she could get in and then scoot it back into place, trapping her right next to Grandpa.

Unfortunately, Aunt Penny was deeply involved in a conversation with Mr. Beiderman, who was sitting on the other side of her. Meanwhile, Grandpa wasn't eating, probably because he had already eaten that slice from the pizza that had fallen to the ground. Grandpa always made her really nervous. He was even quieter than she was, and she never knew what to say to him. She reached out to get a piece of pizza, but just as she was about to put it on her plate, she changed her mind and put it on his plate instead. Then she got another one for herself.

Grandpa didn't acknowledge this, but that was okay with Hyacinth. She didn't really feel like talking anyway, so she listened to the conversations going on around her. Orlando and Oliver were talking about their favorite topic (sports), while Laney and Miss Josie were deep in discussion about how to decorate the garden for Papa's birthday party. Laney wanted to make sure plenty of glitter was involved.

Over on the other side of the table, Isa was trapped in a conversation with Grandma. Polite as always, Isa smiled and nodded and said, "Yes, Grandma." Grandma was drilling her on how many hours she played the violin and what pieces she was working on.

"Your teacher should have you playing more sonatas," Grandma scolded, as if the lack of sonatas were Isa's fault. "How will you improve if you don't play sonatas?"

"I do whatever Mr. Van Hooten tells me to do," Isa told her. "He's the best."

Grandma sniffed, then changed the topic to colleges.

"I'm only a sophomore in high school," Isa said. "I'm not thinking about colleges yet."

"How about George Mason University?" Grandma suggested. "It has a great accounting program.

You're obviously good at math, since you play music. It's only half an hour away from our house. You could live with us and save money."

"Uh, I'm not so sure about being an accountant," Isa said, taking another bite of pizza.

"Your mom was a great accountant," Grandma said to Isa. "She had five accounting firms asking if they could hire her right after she graduated. Five!"

Isa smiled at Grandma. "I might want to go into music."

Grandma looked as if she had eaten something both sour and rotten. "Music? There's no money in music!"

Isa shrugged. "Don't worry about me, Grandma. I have plans."

Hyacinth, secretly thankful that she was not getting drilled by Grandma about her college or career plans, looked across the table to where Jessie and Orlando were sitting.

"Do you think we could make a big balloon drop for Papa's birthday?" Jessie asked Orlando.

"I think so. We need a net and a really tall ladder," Orlando said. "We can hang the net from the trees, and when we're singing 'Happy Birthday,' you can pull a string and the balloons will all fall down around him."

"That sounds great," Jessie said.

Next to Hyacinth, Aunt Penny was *still* talking to Mr. Beiderman. Hyacinth believed they were talking about . . . sea otters?

She leaned toward Aunt Penny, trying to hear her better. Hyacinth *really* liked sea otters.

"Because they're a keystone species," Aunt Penny was telling Mr. Beiderman, "they're really important. They promote the health of the creatures around them by eating urchins and keeping the urchin populations down. Without them, urchins would decimate the giant kelp beds, which are an important habitat for so many creatures. When that happens, species that live in giant kelp suffer, die, and harm the ecosystem."

"How many sea otters live in that area now?" Mr. Beiderman said, his pizza forgotten.

"Nearly three thousand," Aunt Penny said proudly. "Back before 1911, before the sea otters were protected under the North Pacific Fur Seal Treaty, the number around us had dwindled to only fifty."

"Wow," Hyacinth said, and Aunt Penny turned to her.

"Are you interested in oceans?" Aunt Penny asked.

Hyacinth nodded. "I love animals."

Aunt Penny smiled. "I can tell how much you love them by how you take care of Franz and the chickens."

"The New York Aquarium opened up a new shark exhibit," Mr. Beiderman said.

"Oh, I love sharks," Aunt Penny said, turning back to Mr. Beiderman. "They're keystone predators, just like sea otters."

Hyacinth thought about that for a little bit. She had always loved sea otters, but she had never been a fan of sharks. Their little eyes and massive, sharp teeth scared her. But she hadn't known any of that stuff about keystone predators and giant kelp. It sort of made her want to learn more about the oceans, and maybe one day visit that aquarium Aunt Penny worked at.

She took another bite of her pizza, which was now cooled off enough not to burn the roof of her mouth.

She looked toward Grandpa to see how he was doing. His plate was empty, and he had left the table without her noticing.

Hyacinth sighed with relief.

Eleven

Oliver lay on his bed with a copy of *Tristan Strong Punches a Hole in the Sky*, his flashlight illuminating the words on the page. It was after ten o'clock, and the brownstone was happily quiet after the chaos of the day.

The sound of his doorknob turning had him quickly flicking off his flashlight and shoving his book under his pillow. Mama didn't like it when he stayed up too late reading. She said it made him grumpy in the morning, but Oliver honestly didn't see it. He was perfectly pleasant in the mornings.

Oliver tried to make his breath even so Mama wouldn't get suspicious.

"Oliver!"

It was Laney. Oliver sat up.

"What?"

"We're having a family meeting in the basement," she whispered. "But you have to be really quiet. Mama and Aunt Penny are sleeping in the living room."

Oliver climbed out of bed and went down his loft ladder one rung at a time instead of jumping down like he usually did. Together he and Laney descended the stairs, avoiding the three squeaky ones and getting all the way to the bottom without incident.

The sleeper sofa was pulled out, and both Mama and Aunt Penny were fast asleep. Mama hadn't come home until nine o'clock. She ate the leftover cold pizza, changed into borrowed pajamas from Isa, since Grandma and Grandpa had already gone to sleep in her bedroom, and promptly collapsed on the sofa.

Laney and Oliver tiptoed past the slumbering adults, opened the door to the basement, and went underground. Isa, Jessie, and Hyacinth were all there, the twinkle lights making the space glow with a warm light.

"This better be good," Oliver grumbled, slumping down on the carpet. "I'm in the middle of a really good book."

"You're always in the middle of a really good book," Jessie said.

Isa pulled out the letter they had found only that morning. "We haven't had time to talk about Whalers Cove. I did some research on the internet this afternoon. I checked the Whalers Coves in Washington and Oregon, but nothing about them seemed related to World War II. All the stuff that came up in Washington had to do with condominiums and fishing boats."

"I tried to look up Whalers Coves in New York and Massachusetts using Jessie's computer this afternoon," Oliver said, "but then Grandma started bugging me about screen time and I had to stop. The only results that came up had to do with a yacht club and a nursing home."

"I didn't find anything in California," Jessie said. "Hyacinth and Laney, did you find anything in that book you brought home?"

"Nothing in Florida," Hyacinth reported.

"The book is really interesting, though," Laney said.

"You've been reading it?" Isa said, surprised.

Laney nodded.

"I talked to Mrs. Castleman this afternoon," Isa

said, "and even though she knew Pop-Pop, she didn't know about anything about Whalers Cove. But she had some really interesting stories."

"Really?" Hyacinth said. "Tell us."

"I can do better than that," Isa said, pulling out the two photos and her phone. "I recorded it." Isa opened her voice recorder app, and soon they could hear Mrs. Castleman's gentle voice.

Everyone called your grandfather Pop-Pop. The name came from a book he used to read to your dad when he was little. I think it was called *Pop the Porcupine.* We would laugh because whenever your grandfather read it to him, he would point at the porcupine in the picture, then point at your grandfather and yell, "Pop!" Your dad loved that book so much. He carried it with him for a year.

Pop-Pop always had a basketball wedged under his arm. He even brought a ball with him to work just in case the weather was nice and he could play ball with his partner at a nearby court during their lunch breaks. From Monday to Friday, he worked long hours with New York City's Sanitation Department. But on the weekends, he would take your dad to the Harlem YMCA, where he coached a youth basketball league. Your dad did all the drills—even when he was as young as three years old. It was so cute to watch.

Pop-Pop used to go to the parks in the area and watch kids do pickup basketball games. Sometimes he would invite one of the kids to join his team at the YMCA. It was always the kid with the beat-up sneakers or the last kid picked for the team—kids who obviously loved basketball but weren't exactly the stars.

When your dad was little, Pop-Pop brought him to the basketball courts on Fifth Avenue and 135th Street to practice early on Saturday mornings. It was usually deserted except for one person, a kid named Jamal. He was in middle school back then, and he was always around when they got there and stayed after they left. He wasn't great at basketball, but after your grandfather saw him for a few months and gave him pointers, he improved a lot and Pop-Pop invited him to join the rec league at the YMCA.

It was rough in the beginning. I used to go to some of their games, and whenever Jamal played, everyone sort of watched with one hand covering their face. When he was on the court, he would miss a pass or shoot air balls. But Pop-Pop kept working with him, and he got better. A lot better.

Then an opportunity came for Jamal to go to a summer basketball camp for a whole month. The camp gave him a scholarship, but that didn't cover the whole fee. So Pop-Pop hired Jamal to do odd jobs at basketball practice—setup and cleanup, washing the uniforms, that kind of thing. And in return, Pop-Pop paid for his summer camp. When Jamal returned from camp, he had more confidence and more skills, and Pop-Pop moved him to a starting position on the rec league. Jamal continued to attend summer basketball camps—Pop-Pop paying for anything the scholarship didn't cover—and ended up making the high school team and then going on to play on his college's team.

ISA: Where is he now?

MRS. CASTLEMAN: He does something with technology at City College. He still comes in on Saturday mornings, after basketball practice.

ISA: He still plays basketball?

MRS. CASTLEMAN: He actually coaches at the YMCA, just like Pop-Pop. He's there every Saturday.

The recording went quiet, and the Vanderbeekers reacted.

"Wait, what?" Jessie screeched.

"Jamal *coaches* now?" Oliver asked.

"How did we not know this story?" Hyacinth asked. "Papa must know him."

"We need to meet this Jamal guy," Laney said.

Isa smiled. "Mrs. Castleman gave me his number, and I called him after dinner. We're going to meet him on the courts on One Thirty-Fifth Street and Fifth Avenue tomorrow morning."

✦ ✦ ✦

Laney lay in her bed, blinking in the darkness. She had a lot to think about. Even though it was late and Hyacinth and Franz were snoring and Tuxedo was a comforting presence next to her, Laney could not fall asleep.

She was staring at the bottom of the top bunk when the sound of footsteps below jolted her wide awake. The sound traveled across the living room and to the kitchen, and Laney held her breath. Maybe it was a robber! She squeezed into a tight ball, shut her eyes, and waited for Papa to wake up, startle the robber, and chase him from their home. Then she remembered that Papa was very far from the brownstone on 141st Street.

The footsteps continued, and she heard the door that led to the backyard open and close. Then complete silence. Laney opened her eyes and lifted her head. Hyacinth, Franz, and Tuxedo were fast asleep. Who was downstairs? If it was a robber, Laney needed to know. Maybe he had stolen something important, and it was up to her to save the day!

Laney got out of her bed, picked up a very sleepy Tuxedo and put her on her shoulders, then opened her door quietly. She passed the advertisement of her dream bike that she had taped to her door—the bike was red with sparkly silver streamers coming out of the handlebars and a wicker basket attached to the front—and she stood at the top of the stairs. Nothing seemed to be out of place. She stepped down into the kitchen and looked around. Mama and Aunt Penny were still sleeping peacefully, even with a burglar in the brownstone!

A movement in the yard caught Laney's eye through the kitchen window. She made her way to the window and peered out into the darkness. There was Grandpa, standing outside on the grass. He didn't have any shoes on, and he was doing strange movements with slow steps back and forth, his arms circling around his body like bird wings might look in slow motion. She hadn't known he could move like that, and she couldn't stop watching him.

When he came in some time later, she ducked behind the kitchen island so he wouldn't spot her. He stepped back into the brownstone, closed and locked the door behind him, then went across the kitchen and living room and up the stairs.

It was only when she heard his footsteps disappear into Mama and Papa's room that Laney emerged from her hiding spot. Tuxedo jumped to the ground and weaved herself around her ankles, purring. She opened the jar of cat treats they kept on the counter and fed one to her, and George Washington mysteriously appeared at the kitchen island, lured by the sound of food. She fed one to George Washington, and after he ate it he walked back around the corner and vanished.

"Time for bed," Laney whispered to Tuxedo.

As she went up the stairs, she found herself desperately missing her father. She sent a prayer up into the night that he was safe in Indiana. The brownstone felt empty and lonely without his big laugh and big smile.

It didn't matter that there were even more people in their apartment now. No one could replace Papa. The brownstone stairs creaked as she went upstairs and made her way back to bed.

TUESDAY, AUGUST 5

Four Days Until Papa's Birthday

Twelve

The sun was just rising when Hyacinth woke up at six o'clock. She peeked over the side of the top bunk to see what Franz was doing. He was on his back, sound asleep, his tongue hanging from the side of his mouth. She went down the ladder, then leaned over and gently stroked his forehead until he woke up. He rolled to his feet and took his time stretching before standing up and giving a great big yawn.

A clink of dishes made Hyacinth pause. It was odd for someone to be awake already. Usually it was just her and maybe Papa. And if it was Papa, he would be sitting with a book on the couch and drinking coffee, not messing around in the kitchen.

Unfortunately, Franz, hoping for an early breakfast,

bounded toward the kitchen before she could grab his collar. She scrambled downstairs behind him but was too late. He had trotted right up to Grandma and shoved his cold nose into her leg.

Grandma startled and dropped the spoon she was drying.

"Sorry," Hyacinth said in a whisper, not wanting to wake Mama and Aunt Penny, who were still sleeping in the living room. She grabbed Franz's collar before he drooled all over Grandma.

Grandma didn't reply; she just continued doing her thing in the kitchen, occasionally looking uneasily at Franz. She poured some leaves into a delicate green and white teapot that Hyacinth had never seen before. Hyacinth was surprised that her grandma traveled with her own teapot.

"I like your teapot," Hyacinth said.

"It's your mother's teapot," Grandma said. "I gave it to her as a wedding present."

"Really?" Hyacinth said. "I've never seen it before."

"I found it in there," Grandma said, pointing to the cupboard by the door to the backyard.

That was the cupboard where Mama stored things

she didn't use very often, like the waffle iron and the Christmas platter that only came out in December, and things she didn't really want but felt bad throwing out, like the huge oven mitts shaped like bear paws that Mr. Jones had given her for her fortieth birthday.

"Tea?" Grandma asked.

"No, thanks," Hyacinth said. "I've got to take Franz out."

Grandma glanced quickly at Hyacinth but didn't reply, and a moment later she was busy again with her tea making. Hyacinth grabbed Papa's light jacket off the hook, picked up the scraps bucket, and accompanied Franz into the backyard. The grass was damp and soggy from the previous day's rain. She unlatched the chicken coop, and the chickens scrambled all over one another to get out.

Hyacinth poured the scraps on the ground in front of their coop, then put the bucket by the back door. She sat on the side of the porch while Franz snuffled around. She didn't want to go back inside and face Grandma, so she stayed outside. She watched as the sky grew lighter and the sun cast a golden glow on the brownstones and the chickens wandered happily after Franz. Her thoughts drifted to the teapot, and she wondered if Grandma was bothered by the fact that Mama didn't use it. It looked like a really nice teapot.

Her peace was interrupted when Oliver emerged, the screen door banging when he came out.

He took a seat next to Hyacinth.

"Hey," he said.

"Hi," she replied. "You're up early."

"Grandma's phone went off, and the ringer was so loud that it woke everyone up."

Hyacinth nodded.

"Jimmy L and his mom are out of town," Oliver observed. "Maybe we could move into their apartment until our grandparents leave."

"I like his place," Hyacinth said. "I like all the nesting dolls in the living room." Ms. Lim had a collection of 145 nesting dolls from all over the world.

"I wonder why Grandma and Grandpa are even here," Oliver said. "Don't you think it's strange that they came out of the blue?'

Hyacinth nodded, because she did find it odd. But she also found herself wondering about that teapot and the look Grandma gave her when she'd declined the offer of tea. It reminded her of the look she had seen on her friend's face last year when she said she was moving away—sad but resigned.

"We better get going," Oliver said, looking at his watch. "We're supposed to meet Jamal in an hour."

Hyacinth whistled for Franz and smiled as he galloped toward her, his ears flapping in the wind and his tongue hanging out. He crashed into her knees, and Hyacinth couldn't help but laugh as she wrapped her arms around her dear friend, absorbing his comfort before they headed into the brownstone.

❁ ❁ ❁

When Oliver and Hyacinth came back, everyone was gathered in the kitchen and dining room. Mama was at the stove making breakfast; Aunt Penny was sitting on a stool by the kitchen island, a cup of coffee cradled in her hands; Grandpa was fixing the broken staircase spindle; and Laney was practicing her bike riding around the living and dining areas.

Aunt Penny yawned and shifted her legs so Laney could bike by. "This time change is brutal."

"What time is it in California?" Oliver asked.

"Five in the morning."

"That's Hyacinth's usual wake-up time," Oliver commented.

"I usually wake up at six," Hyacinth corrected her brother.

"It's *so* early," Oliver said. "It's inhuman."

"I admire people who can wake up early," Aunt Penny said. "I think there was a study done about how people who wake up early are more productive."

"Really?" Jessie asked, rubbing the sleep out of her eyes. "What study was that?"

"Hyacinth is the most productive person I know," Oliver said. "Last week, I woke up on a Saturday and Hyacinth had already baked dog biscuits, mended a shirt I tore during a basketball game, and knitted a hat."

Aunt Penny's eyebrows rose. "That's impressive." Then she took another sip of coffee.

Grandma was sitting at the dining room table, waiting for breakfast while also trying to avoid getting bumped into by Laney on her bike.

"We usually eat breakfast at six thirty," Grandma said.

Oliver glanced at the clock that hung on the wall in the kitchen. It was eight o'clock.

"This is actually early for us," Oliver said. "We don't eat breakfast at six thirty unless it's a school day."

Grandma looked as if she wanted to reply to that, but Mama came by with a tub of yogurt and homemade granola with honeyed oats, nuts, and dried cherries.

"Breakfast is ready!" she said as Isa brought a stack of bowls to the table and Jessie set down a mug filled with spoons.

"What is this?" Grandma asked, pointing to the dishes Mama had just put on the table.

"Granola! My favorite!" Laney said, pushing Oliver's hand away so she could get at the granola before he did.

"I love this stuff," Jessie said, grabbing another serving spoon so she didn't have to wait for everyone else to serve themselves.

The Vanderbeeker kids, knowing that it would soon be time to meet Jamal, scarfed down their breakfast while Aunt Penny shook her head with amusement.

"I don't know how you keep up with so many hungry kids," Aunt Penny said.

"They're usually not so wolflike in their eating," Mama said, observing them.

"Growth spurts?" Aunt Penny inquired.

"They're always in a growth spurt."

"Jessie is, at least," Oliver said around a mouthful of granola. "She's a giant."

"Unkind, Oliver," Isa remarked, throwing a balled-up napkin at him. He ducked, and it missed him and bonked Franz's nose on the way down. Franz gobbled up the napkin before anyone could get it.

"Good one, Isa," Oliver said. "Now he's going to throw up."

Grandma looked at them for a long moment. Then she poured another cup of tea for herself. Neither she nor Grandpa made a move to get something to eat.

Done inhaling their breakfast, the Vanderbeeker kids rinsed their dishes and stacked them in the dishwasher.

"We've got to meet someone at the basketball courts," Jessie said.

Mama peered at her children. "All of you?"

"All of us," Oliver said. "I'm going to, uh, show everyone my moves."

That wasn't technically a lie. He did plan on playing a little basketball, as long as they were there.

"We'll be back in an hour," Isa told Aunt Penny. "You can think about what you want to do today."

"Can I come with you?" Aunt Penny asked. "I want to see Oliver's sweet basketball moves."

"Well . . ." Isa said slowly. "It's probably going to be boring."

Even though he knew they weren't sharing their plans about Pop-Pop and the letter with anyone, Oliver's pride was too fragile to let that comment pass. "I wouldn't say it's *boring*. I mean, I think I'm a pretty exciting basketball player—"

"I'm just saying you might want to rest," Isa interrupted. "Enjoy your coffee. Take a nap."

"Actually," Aunt Penny said, "a walk would wake me up."

Oliver sighed. They couldn't say no, right?

Thirteen

The Vanderbeekers plus Aunt Penny headed to the basketball court around eight forty-five. They were supposed to meet Jamal at nine. Laney insisted on riding her bike, even though it made Isa nervous and she constantly had to shout for Laney to slow down or watch out.

There were only two people at the court. One person was in a wheelchair shooting baskets from the free throw line and sinking every ball. The other person was standing under the backboard, retrieving the balls and throwing them back.

Oliver gaped. "That guy has not missed one basket!"

Laney walked right up to the guy shooting baskets. "Are you Jamal?"

He smiled at her and turned his wheelchair to face her. "I am. Are you the Vanderbeekers?"

"We are!" Laney said. "Plus Aunt Penny. She's a Chung, though, not a Vanderbeeker."

"Hello to the Vanderbeekers and one Chung," Jamal said. "It's good to meet you all."

"Hello!" Aunt Penny said, stepping close to shake Jamal's hand. She then noticed a coffee cart across the street. "Ooh, coffee. Does anyone else want coffee?" She looked at Jamal and raised her eyebrows.

"I'm good," he said.

"Okay, I'll be right back."

The guy who had been under the basket walked over.

"And this is my son, David," Jamal added. "He's starting college this fall."

"And all Dad wants to do is play basketball until I leave," David said, punching his dad lightly on the arm. He looked at Oliver and Laney curiously. "Your skin is speckled with red and green."

Oliver held his hands up sheepishly. "Food coloring experiment."

After the Vanderbeekers introduced themselves,

David joined a pickup game with a few guys who entered the court while Jamal and the Vanderbeekers headed toward the wide concrete steps that served as bleachers. Jamal rolled to a stop in front of them.

"It's amazing to meet Pop-Pop's grandchildren," Jamal said. "I can't believe I haven't met you before."

"We're so glad to meet *you*," Isa said. Then she explained how none of them had ever met Pop-Pop and were trying to learn more about him.

"Pop-Pop was like a father to me," Jamal told them. "He changed my life."

"Mrs. Castleman told us that he asked you to join the YMCA league and you got really good and went on to play in high school and college," Isa said.

"I want to play college basketball," Oliver said. "My coach lets me and my friends work out with his high school team in the mornings, even though I'm only in middle school."

"You must be really good," Jamal said.

"I'm working on it," Oliver said. "Were you in a wheelchair back when you knew our grandfather?"

Jamal nodded. "Yes, but it was after I had known him for many years. I was in college and our basketball team was traveling to an away game. Our van was sideswiped by a tractor trailer."

"That's terrible," Hyacinth said.

"It was terrible," Jamal agreed. "It was my junior year in college and we were having a great season. The crash changed everything. I spent two months in the hospital, but Pop-Pop visited every day. When I was finally discharged, I didn't want to leave my apartment. My mom was working three jobs to keep us afloat, so I was alone all the time. Pop-Pop, though, he stopped by every day after work before he picked your dad up from school. And then, a few months after the accident, he started coming by on Saturday mornings. And one Saturday, without any warning, he picked me up and carried me down the three flights of stairs while your dad hauled my wheelchair down the building stairs."

"Pop-Pop must have been really strong!" Jessie said.

"He was," Jamal said with a grin. "Although we always made fun of him for being old."

Jamal continued to share how Pop-Pop took him to the courts and how much he hated it. He would sit in his wheelchair and pretend he was somewhere else. After three months, one Saturday Pop-Pop looked at him and passed the ball. Jamal caught it without thinking and took a shot. Even though he had missed by a mile, Pop-Pop threw the ball back to him. He kept on missing, but eventually started making some baskets. Then, after a year of physical therapy, Jamal joined a recreational wheelchair basketball team, then an amateur basketball team, and amazingly was even an alternate on the USA Paralympic wheelchair basketball team a few years later.

"That's incredible," Isa said.

"Pop-Pop watched every single game live on television, and there was always a message from him afterward. He loved basketball so much."

"Just like Oliver," Hyacinth said.

"And just like your dad," Jamal said.

"I had no idea that Pop-Pop played," Oliver said. "And I can't believe you were at the Olympics."

Jamal looked at Oliver. "Life is a peculiar and mysterious thing," he said. "Sometimes one moment changes a life forever."

"What was our dad like back then?" Jessie asked.

"I didn't know your dad that well. We were eight years apart, so by the time he was in middle school, I was in college. But from what I know of him, he's just like your grandfather. A strong, noble man with a wonderful heart."

"Papa is the best," Laney declared.

"We found a letter our grandfather wrote to our dad," Isa said. "It was right before our dad's graduation. He talked about a trip they were going to make. Do you know anything about it?"

Jamal nodded. "I remember Pop-Pop telling me that he was surprising Derek with a trip. He was so excited about it. It was going to be the first time they'd traveled together since he had started college. Their trip was a month long, so he asked me to coach the basketball league while he was gone."

"What did you know about the trip?" Oliver asked.

"Not much. Just that he wanted to see a place by the ocean. I had just gotten a new job and was working long hours, so I didn't see him very often in those few months when he was planning the trip."

"Do you have any idea who would know more about it?"

Jamal thought. "I think his best friend from the sanitation department is still around. They were partners on their collection route for a decade. If there's anyone around who might know about it, it would be him. They were two peas in a pod."

"Do you know his name?" Isa asked.

"Sure do. Yardsy Loughty."

"Yard-see what?" Laney asked.

Jamal spelled it, and Isa typed it into her phone.

"I don't have his contact information, but maybe you can find it online."

"Thank you," Isa said.

"Any more questions?" Jamal asked.

"I have one," Oliver said. "Can we play basketball now?"

☼ ☼ ☼

It wasn't long after they started their basketball game that Aunt Penny returned, coffee in hand.

"I just had the most fascinating conversation with the guy at the coffee cart—"

"Get on a team!" Oliver yelled.

"Okay!" Aunt Penny said as she set down her coffee. "Where should I go?"

"Over there," Oliver said, pointing to the other group. He was with Jamal, Isa, and Hyacinth.

Aunt Penny jogged over to Jessie, Laney, and David, who had finished his pickup game. "Did I tell you I'm on the recreational basketball team at work? And I'm really competitive."

"Perfect!" Jessie said.

"What do I need to know about the other team?" Aunt Penny asked.

"Keep an eye on Hyacinth. She's deceptively good because she helps Oliver with his drills."

"Good to know," Aunt Penny said as she did some quick hamstring stretches.

"Also, Jamal played for the United States Paralympics basketball team."

"We're toast," Aunt Penny said.

From the other side of the court, Oliver yelled, "You ready to play or are you scared?"

"And Oliver loves to trash-talk," Jessie added.

They played for an hour with no break. The score

was close, but Oliver's team won. After all, they had a former Olympian playing with them.

"Next time *we* get Jamal," Laney said.

"How about we give you Isa instead?" Oliver said.

"Not Isa!" Laney protested.

"Hey," Isa said. "I'm not even supposed to play basketball. Mr. Van Hooten doesn't want me to jam my fingers."

"So *that* explains why you never caught the ball whenever I passed to you," Jamal said.

Everyone was sweaty and hungry, so Aunt Penny took a bag of apples from her backpack and passed them around.

"Can we do this again?" Oliver asked Jamal. He used his shirt to wipe away the sweat.

"I'm here every Saturday morning," Jamal said.

"Thanks for everything," Isa said. "We really appreciate you telling us about Pop-Pop."

"I feel like we're getting to know him," Laney said.

Jamal smiled. "Your grandfather was the best of men. I hope you know that and are proud of it."

"If you're not doing anything this Saturday, you

should come by our dad's birthday party," Oliver said. "It's at the community garden on 141st Street near Frederick Douglass Boulevard. Three o'clock."

"There's going to be a balloon drop!" Laney told him.

"Maybe we will," Jamal said. "It's been a long time."

Fourteen

Aunt Penny wanted to see the cat café on the way home, so they stopped by for ten minutes to say hi to Mama, grab a cookie, meet the cats, and get Aunt Penny *another* cup of coffee.

"I'm on a three-hour time difference, people!" she said.

On the walk home, Aunt Penny could not stop talking about Mama's café.

"I just love those cat siblings! Did you see them sleeping in that cat bed shaped like a hamburger?" Aunt Penny exclaimed. "And that cat with the really smooshed-up face! Just adorable!"

"Do you have a pet?" Laney asked.

"I wish," Aunt Penny said. "I would love a cat or a dog."

"You should adopt one!" Hyacinth said.

"I work so much," Aunt Penny said. "I would feel bad leaving a pet home alone for so long."

"Cats are pretty independent," Oliver said. "George Washington *wants* to be left alone."

"You could get the sibling cats," Laney suggested. "They would keep each other company while you're at work."

"Their names are Peaches and Cream," Hyacinth said. "We love them!"

"How would I get them back to California?" Aunt Penny asked.

"You could get a cat carrier and bring them on the

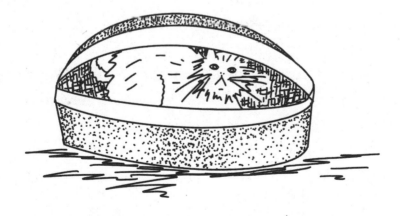

plane," Laney suggested. "I like those bubble back-packs where there's a plastic piece so the pets can look out. I have one for Tuxedo."

"That's nice," Aunt Penny said, then changed the topic. "So what are we going to do today?"

"We have to do some research on a person who knew our grandfather," Isa told her. "Papa's dad, who we nev-er met because he died when Papa was in college."

"Oh, I remember that," Aunt Penny said. "Your mom was so sad. I'm sorry you never got to know him."

"We're trying to find out more about him," Laney told her.

"I can help," Aunt Penny offered.

"You don't have to," Jessie said. "You came here for vacation. You probably want to go out and have fun, not try to track down random people who knew Pop-Pop."

Aunt Penny shrugged. "I've got all week. Anyway, a big part of coming here was to spend time with you all and redeem myself as the 'cool aunt.'"

"Like Auntie Harrigan?" Laney asked. "We love her."

"She does have the distinct advantage of having

lived near you for your entire lives," Aunt Penny said. "It's hard to top that."

"You could take us to a Knicks game at Madison Square Garden," Oliver said.

"Or skydiving," Jessie suggested.

"Or let us help you adopt two adorable, homeless cats," Hyacinth said.

"I'll get back to you about that," Aunt Penny said. "But you should probably lower your expectations."

The Vanderbeekers approached the brownstone, all looking forward to getting on the computer to look up Yardsy Loughty. If they had any chance of putting together a trip for Papa by Saturday, only four days away, they needed to talk to him as soon as possible. Jessie stuck her key into the door, but before she could turn it, the door swung open to reveal Grandma and Grandpa.

"Where have you been?" Grandma demanded. "We didn't come all the way to New York City to be stuck in this apartment!"

"You could have gone out on your own—" Oliver began.

"We don't know *how* to get around New York

City," Grandma snapped. "We don't want to be robbed or killed."

"Grandma," Jessie said as she stood in the living room, puzzled by Grandma's sudden display of concern, "New York City is one of the safest large cities in the world."

Grandma shook her head again. "I don't know why your parents let you run around like delinquents."

"We're very responsible," Isa told her.

"And we know a million people in the neighborhood," Laney added.

"Mama and Papa trust us," Jessie said. "And if we need them, we just call."

Grandma shook her head. "Never mind. Today you will take us to the Brooklyn Bridge."

"I thought you were scared of going out into New York City," Oliver pointed out.

"Grandma, there's actually something we need to do right now," Jessie began.

But Grandma's mouth was set in a straight line. "Grandpa wants to go to the Brooklyn Bridge. We will go."

⚙ ⚙ ⚙

The last time the Vanderbeekers had gone to the Brooklyn Bridge, Laney was three years old, and she managed to create a fifty-three-bike pile-up in the bike lane. It had been a hot summer day, and the Vanderbeekers plus Miss Josie, Mr. Jeet, Auntie Harrigan, and Uncle Arthur had planned a lovely afternoon. They headed downtown on the number 2 subway train and got off in Brooklyn, where they walked by beautiful brownstones on gorgeous, tree-shaded streets.

It was the middle of the afternoon by the time they had stepped onto the bridge, and the Vanderbeekers were getting tired. After a few wrong turns, they finally found the entrance and got on the pedestrian walkway, joining thousands of overheated and grumpy tourists who had also thought that walking across the Brooklyn Bridge was a good idea.

The pedestrian walkway had a thick white line painted right in the middle, which separated pedestrians and bikers. Unfortunately, with so many people angling to take the best photos on the bridge, it became impossible to have a nice, leisurely walk. Instead, Mama and Papa were constantly reminding the kids to watch out or to stay in the pedestrian lane and not step into the bike lane.

Laney had the worst time of it. Being only thirty-one and a half inches tall at the time, she was often invisible to zealous photographers who swung their bags over their shoulders and accidentally smacked her in the face or who hit the back of her head while raising a selfie stick. Thirty minutes later, the Vanderbeekers and their friends were hot and sweaty and grouchy — and they were only halfway across the bridge.

"How much longer?" Laney had asked, looking up at Papa.

"We're almost to the end," Papa said, scanning the crowds to make sure all his kids were still accounted for.

At just that moment, a bike passed over into the pedestrian lane. The rubber handgrip hit Laney in the back, and she fell down. The bike and the biker continued on without so much as an apology. Papa didn't see it happen—he had just noticed that Oliver was nowhere to be seen—and Laney got up and took one big step into the bike lane.

"Watch it!" yelled a man on a sleek black bike who swerved around her.

"Get out of the bike lane!" yelled a woman who zipped past her.

But Laney had had enough. She continued into the bike lane and reached her arms out as far as they could go, effectively blocking bikers from passing her. Unfortunately, a bike tour group from France, who were all wearing matching T-shirts with the French flag embroidered on the pocket, were in a tight group and heading right toward her. The leader, who had a flag hanging from her bike basket, was saying something to the person behind her as she gestured toward the Manhattan skyline.

She didn't see Laney standing tall and angry in the middle of the bike path, daring cyclists to run her over. At the very last moment, the French tour leader glimpsed Laney, swiveled her handlebars, and ended up crashing into the side of the bridge and falling down. This subsequently caused a massive collision of the entire fifty-three-person tour group, which led to lots of angry French words spoken as the leader searched for the person responsible.

Fortunately, she only caught a quick glimpse of Laney before she rammed into the side rail, and Laney, scrambling back over to the pedestrian side to avoid being run over, had become enveloped in the crowds of people.

"There you are!" Papa said. "I lost track of Oliver, and by the time I found him, there was this huge bike crash and I couldn't see you and I thought you had somehow gotten in the middle of it. Our relaxing walk across the Brooklyn Bridge hasn't been so relaxing, has it?"

And so Papa lifted her onto his shoulders and they headed toward the Manhattan side of the bridge. When they were a safe distance away, Laney looked back to see the tour leader scanning the crowds for her. Laney quickly turned away and vowed to tell no one about her role in the Great Bike Pile-Up on the Brooklyn Bridge.

That was the memory that flashed through Laney's mind when Grandma said the words "Brooklyn Bridge."

"How about we go to City College instead?" Laney suggested. "It's pretty there."

Grandma shook her head vigorously. "Brooklyn Bridge. That is where Grandpa wants to go."

Laney looked at Grandpa. It did not look as if he had any preference for the bridge whatsoever.

"Ugh, Brooklyn," Oliver muttered. He was not fond of long subway rides.

Isa cleared her throat. "It's probably going to be crowded. It's very popular with tourists."

"Remember the last time we went to the bridge?" Jessie said. "We lost both Oliver and Laney."

"You didn't *lose* me," Oliver said. "I was just stuck behind a bunch of people and no one could see me."

"I wasn't lost either," Laney said. "I was there the whole time."

"Papa lost track of you and freaked out," Isa told her.

"We are going to the Brooklyn Bridge," Grandma said firmly and loudly. Then she took Grandpa's hand and marched right out the front door, and there was nothing for the Vanderbeekers and Aunt Penny to do but follow.

Fifteen

For Jessie, the ride down to Brooklyn felt much longer than it actually was. This was because they first had to convince Grandma that the subway was safe.

She had initially refused to go down the stairs, proclaiming them "dirty." Jessie could see that she was torn between her deep desire to go to the Brooklyn Bridge (which Jessie could not understand) and her distaste for the New York City subway.

"Grandma, do you want to go home?" Jessie asked with the infinite patience required of a botanist studying the growth rate of Arctic moss. "It's fine if you're not comfortable with the subway. We can go home if you like."

The threat of not going to the Brooklyn Bridge

must have been enough to finally convince Grandma to steel herself. She set her eyes on the stairs and marched her way down to the station. Everyone followed her, and Isa distributed MetroCards.

When the train arrived, it was crowded, but they managed to find a car empty enough to squeeze their big group inside.

"Hold on to the pole," Jessie said to Grandma and Grandpa. Grandpa obeyed, but Grandma hesitated. She was looking at the pole as if someone had just licked it.

"Germs," Grandma said, but then the subway lurched and Grandma stumbled.

Jessie tried to grab her before she fell, but missed. Grandma fell right into the lap of a guy who looked as if he were a professional weightlifter. He wore a tight T-shirt, and his arm muscles bulged. From the top of the shirt emerged a tattooed snake that coiled around his neck and ended just below his left ear. The man wore a black hat with white stitching that said "What Are YOU Looking At?"

"Sorry, sorry," Grandma said, her face blooming with color.

The man looked at her and grinned. "Glad I could

break your fall." He helped her back to her feet, then stood and offered her his seat. Because he was so broad, he actually opened up two seats when he rose, and Laney jumped at the chance to sit in the other one.

"Thank you," Grandma said.

"You're all red," Laney told her.

"It's a reaction of the sympathetic nervous system," Jessie told her. "When you're embarrassed, adrenaline is released, speeding up your heart rate and dilating your blood vessels to improve blood flow and oxygen delivery."

"Don't be embarrassed," said the tattooed weight-lifter. "It happens to me all the time."

"Really?" Laney said, looking at him. "You fall into people's laps in the subway?"

"Not really," he said, smiling at her. "I just said that to make her feel better."

"That's sweet," Aunt Penny said.

Grandma nodded at him. "Thank you."

"We're going to the Brooklyn Bridge," Laney told him. "I like your tattoo."

"Thanks," he said. "Snakes represent the creative life force in all of us."

"Huh," Oliver said. "I'm going to tell Mama that. She has a thing about snakes."

"She'll *never* let you get a snake," Jessie said. "It's the ophidiophobia."

"What's oh-phee-phobia?" Laney asked.

"An abnormal fear of snakes," the tattooed weightlifter replied. "It's a shame that so many people experience that, because snakes are actually symbols of rebirth, transformation, immortality, and healing."

"I'm going to get a snake tattoo when I grow up," Oliver decided.

"Me too!" Laney declared.

"Brooklyn Bridge, huh?" the weightlifter said to Grandma. "It's gotten mighty crowded there. Be careful you don't get knocked out by a selfie stick."

"I will be careful," she assured him.

"There's a nice pizza place right around the entrance on the Brooklyn side," he said.

"Patsy's Pizzeria?" Jessie said. "We've been there before."

"No, there's another place, a little hole in the wall called Brazo's Pizzeria. My friend owns it. He mills his own flour in the basement, and there's a wood-burning oven that makes the best crust. It's on the corner of Bridge and Johnson Streets."

"We will go there," Grandma assured him. "Isa, write it down."

Isa typed the name and location into her phone.

"Where did you get your tattoo?" Oliver asked innocently.

The man pulled his wallet from his back pocket, retrieved a business card, and handed it to Oliver. "This is my buddy's tattoo parlor. It's in the West Village. Tell him Silver sent you."

"Whoa, thanks," Oliver said, cradling the business card like a newborn bird.

"Your name is Silver?" Laney said.

The man nodded.

"I wish my name was Silver," Laney said wistfully.

"Well, this is my stop," Silver said. "Nice to meet you all. Don't forget—Brazo's Pizzeria!" The crowd parted so he could get to the exit.

"Thank you," Grandma called again. She turned to the Vanderbeekers. "That is a nice gentleman."

"I can't believe he gave me this card," Oliver said.

Grandma turned her eyes on Oliver. "No tattoos,

Oliver." She held her hand out, wiggling her fingers for the business card.

"You just said Silver was a nice gentleman!" Oliver protested.

"That does not mean you must get a snake tattoo," Grandma said, her fingers still wiggling.

"Life is so unfair," Oliver said with a huff, giving up the card.

"Hey!" said another passenger, poking Grandpa's shoulder. "Want to sit down? There's an open seat."

Grandpa nodded and made his way to the open seat, the passenger taking his arm for balance on the bouncy subway. Slowly, more people started standing up so Aunt Penny and the Vanderbeeker kids could sit down. Even when Isa said she was fine standing, a woman wearing a white suit and three-inch heels insisted that she take her seat.

"New Yorkers are very nice," Grandma said, looking around at the assortment of people, some snoozing, some listening to their headphones, and others reading to pass the commute time. They were young and old, with long straight hair and dreadlocks and perms, in clothes that were mostly black but with a handful of people wearing color as well. The subway rumbled its way through the pulsing, churning city, under skyscrapers and streets bustling with pedestrians and dogs getting their walks and babies being pushed in strollers.

"I think you like the subway," Laney told Grandma.

Grandma didn't respond, but Jessie thought she saw the beginnings of a smile playing on her lips when their eyes met.

✦ ✦ ✦

Of all the Vanderbeeker kids, Hyacinth liked crowds the least. Sometimes people were surprised to hear that Hyacinth loved living in Harlem, since New York City was one of the largest cities in the world. But each individual neighborhood was different, and 141st Street was relatively peaceful compared to other parts of New York City.

The Brooklyn Bridge in the middle of a beautiful Sunday afternoon?

Not so peaceful.

Hyacinth was glad to sit next to Aunt Penny on the ride down to Brooklyn. Grandma seemed a little friendlier since falling into the lap of the tattooed man, but Grandpa was as silent as the moon. Even though Hyacinth herself was quiet, she preferred to be around people who talked a lot. That meant she could listen, which made her happy.

When they finally got to their stop, Hyacinth made sure to stay near Aunt Penny so she wouldn't be stuck walking with Grandma or Grandpa. Isa led the way to the pizza place that Silver had recommended, Brazo's Pizzeria. Since it was the middle of the afternoon and after the lunch rush, there wasn't much of a crowd, which was good because the place was tiny and their group took up half the seats in the restaurant.

Hyacinth breathed a sigh of relief when she was able to snag the chair farthest away from her grandparents. She swallowed a feeling of guilt over the fact that she didn't enjoy being around them. These thoughts quickly disappeared with the chaos of ordering enough pizza for eight people with a variety of opinions about toppings. Finally, they settled on two large pies, one that was all cheese and the other one half spinach and artichoke and half pineapple and tomatoes (Laney's favorite).

Hyacinth helped Isa pour water from big pitchers that someone brought to their table, and by the time they had mopped up the large glass of ice water Laney knocked over, the pizzas had arrived. Hot from the wood-burning oven and still steaming, the pizzas had beautiful golden crusts that were slightly charred in spots. The group dug in, hungry from their busy day, and it wasn't long before everyone was happy and full.

The owner came out of the kitchen, his apron smeared with sauce and his arms smudged with flour.

"Good?" he inquired as he observed the empty metal pans.

"Yes!" they all chorused.

"A guy on the subway told us about you," Laney informed him. "His name is Silver."

The owner laughed. "Silver is one of my best friends. He's here at least twice a week, and he's always sending new customers our way."

"We're going to tell everyone we know about this place," Laney said.

"Thank you," he said to her. "And for that, you get this"—he pulled a disposable paper hat from his apron pocket, opened it up, and put it on her head—"and this." He went to a display of red T-shirts that said "Brazo's Pizzeria: A Pie to Die For," plucked a kid's-sized one, and handed it to her.

"Wow, thank you!" Laney said, and promptly put it on over her dress.

He smiled. "Free advertising!"

Aunt Penny insisted on paying for lunch, and while she did, the Vanderbeekers got their stuff together and used the restroom. That was why no one but Hyacinth noticed that Grandpa had quietly snuck out the door. She tried to follow him, but she was in a seat on the far side of the table against the wall, and she had to climb over Laney tying her sneakers in order to make it to the front door.

By the time she got there, Grandpa had disappeared.

Sixteen

As usual, Isa did a head count upon leaving the pizzeria.

"One, two, three four, five, six, seven, eight . . . ," Isa counted, looking at their group. "Wait, who are we missing?"

Hyacinth spoke up immediately. "Grandpa. I saw him leave when Aunt Penny was paying for lunch."

"He just . . . left?" Aunt Penny asked.

"That's what it looked like," Hyacinth said. "But by the time I got to the door, he had disappeared."

Everyone looked at Grandma. She shrugged. "He disappears sometimes. But he always comes back."

"I promised Mama I wouldn't lose anyone," said Isa, who had texted Mama before getting on the subway.

It was one thing to be lost in Harlem, where they knew so many people, but Brooklyn was an entirely different issue. She imagined telling Mama that they had lost Grandpa and all they knew was that he was somewhere in Brooklyn.

"I wish he carried a cell phone," Jessie said.

"Even if he had one, he wouldn't know how to use it," Grandma said.

"We should split up and look for him," Isa said.

"Great idea," Aunt Penny said.

They split into two groups: Isa, Grandma, Hyacinth, and Laney would look for Grandpa around the pizzeria, while Jessie, Aunt Penny, and Oliver would trace their steps back to the subway.

"I hope he didn't go back to the subway," Jessie said, urging Aunt Penny and Oliver to run with her. "He'll be lost forever."

Isa was worried. There were so many places Grandpa could be. She popped her head back into Brazo's Pizzeria to give them her number and ask them to call if Grandpa showed up. They walked toward the entrance to the Brooklyn Bridge. They passed huge offices and residential buildings alongside smaller stores, pharmacies, and a little doughnut shop that Laney was very interested in. They passed dads with babies strapped to their chests and families with kids wearing day camp T-shirts and couples jogging together and friends carrying paper cups of coffee and chatting. But no Grandpa.

Isa took her phone and sent a note to Jessie. "Any Grandpa sightings?" she wrote.

The answer was instant. "No."

"Isa!" Laney yelled, pointing toward the entrance to the bridge. "I see him! He's over there!"

Isa squinted at the man Laney was pointing at. "That's just someone who looks like Grandpa," Isa said. "That guy is renting bikes to tourists who want to ride across the bridge."

But Laney was already off and running.

☼ ☼ ☼

Laney ran right up to Grandpa. He was surrounded by bikes.

"Are you helping that man rent bikes?" Laney asked, pointing at the racks and racks of bikes in front of a big sign that said "Bike the Brooklyn Bridge!

Pick up here, drop off on the Manhattan side!"

Grandpa shook his head. "These are for us."

Laney glanced at the bikes, saw that there were eight set apart from the others, then looked at her grandpa. She was so surprised and happy that she hugged him around the waist. "This is the best!"

Grandpa was stiff for a moment but soon relaxed into the hug and patted Laney awkwardly on the head. She was so excited about the biking that she didn't mind the head pat.

"Wow, Grandpa," Isa said. "Did you rent bikes for all of us? That's awesome, but hey, can you let us know ahead of time if you're going to disappear?"

Isa pulled out her phone and texted Jessie. "Found Grandpa. Meet us at the bridge entrance."

"I'm glad we found him," Grandma said when she reached them. "One time he left the house, got on the wrong bus, and ended up three hours away in a different state."

"Ooh, tell us that story, Grandma," Laney said.

Jessie's voice came from down the street. "Hey! You found him!" She was jogging toward them with Oliver and Aunt Penny right behind her.

"Wow, bikes. Cool," Oliver said when he arrived and surveyed the scene. "You just made Laney's entire year."

"Grandma was about to tell us a story of when Grandpa got lost. Like, really lost. Not just disappearing to rent us all bikes," Laney said.

"Later," Grandma said before gracefully hopping onto a bike.

There was only one bike that Laney would be able to ride, and it was literally her dream bike—almost exactly the bike from the picture she had taped to her bedroom door. The bike was red with sparkly silver streamers coming out of the handlebars, and the seat was made of soft red leather. A wicker basket was attached to the front. She ran to it and jumped on. It wasn't too small or too big—it was just right for her.

"Put on the helmet!" Isa hollered.

Laney strapped on the helmet—it too was red, with black polka dots, and looked like a ladybug—and put her feet on the pedals. After wobbling for a few seconds, she did a few laps around the fountain in the park. Her knees weren't even close to hitting the handlebars!

"This is the best bike ever!" she yelled as she went by, her hair blowing back in the wind. She felt like she was flying! After seven laps around the fountain, she headed back to Grandpa and braked to a stop a few inches away from him. She leaned over and hugged him again.

The rest of the Vanderbeekers, Grandpa, Grandma, and Aunt Penny strapped on their helmets and mounted their bikes, and away they went. The bike lane was a lot less crowded than the pedestrian lane, and Grandpa led the way onto the path, followed by Laney, Grandma, the rest of the kids, and then Aunt Penny bringing up the rear.

"This is awesome!" Laney yelled as they passed tourist after tourist on the walkway. Her bike had a bell on it, so whenever someone stepped over into the bike lane, she rang the bell and the pedestrian stepped back into their lane. It was like magic!

Seeing New York City from the Brooklyn Bridge on bikes was a million times better than walking. The breeze felt good on her face, and the city skyline sparkled in the afternoon sun. She could see boats in the harbor and the orange Staten Island ferry bringing people back and forth between the Manhattan and Staten Island terminals. Behind her, she could hear faint peals of laughter from her siblings, and every so often, her grandfather would turn his head and raise his eyebrows at her, as if to say *Having fun?*

She would smile back at him, hoping her smile showed how special this was. But biking was a lot faster than walking, and too soon they reached the Manhattan side of the bridge. Grandpa stopped, and Laney braked behind him. He looked at her, and then pointed back toward the Brooklyn side, as if to say *Again?*

Laney didn't think she could smile any bigger. He took that as a yes, and he gestured for her to go first this time. She turned the bike around and back they went. She saw the surprised faces of her siblings as they figured out they were going back across, but they smiled and turned their bikes toward Brooklyn.

The view of Brooklyn was quite beautiful. As they got closer to the borough, they could peek over the bridge and get a look at the park. There was a gorgeous carousel right by the water, and as they got closer, they could see the box of glass encasing it. The wooden horses were resplendent in their majestic sad-

dles, their heads tossed back and their tails swishing. And when they got to the Brooklyn side, they had a choice to either leave the bikes at the rental place or go back to the Manhattan side.

Laney looked at Grandpa, and when he raised his eyebrows, she grinned and took off back toward Manhattan, just as the colors of the afternoon began to shift to evening hues and the sun cast a rosy glow over the city. And when they all rolled the bikes down the bridge and to the rental place on the Manhattan side, Laney was stopped as she tried to put her bike on the return rack.

"That's not our bike," the rental employee said.

Laney's eyes widened. "What do you mean?"

"You can't leave that here. It's not one of our bikes."

Laney glanced around at the other bikes that her family was leaving on the bike racks. They were scuffed and dented, with black plastic baskets in the front and stickers that said "NYC Bike Tours" slapped on the frame. The bike she had been riding was shiny and new with no stickers. She looked around for Grandpa, but she could only see his back; he was already half a block away, heading toward the subway with Isa.

Seventeen

It was a boisterous subway ride back to Harlem. The Vanderbeekers were reinvigorated by their bike ride across the Brooklyn Bridge. Laney had thanked Grandpa seventeen times, then spent the rest of the time showing her bike to fellow subway riders.

Jessie hadn't heard from Papa all day, so when the train paused at a station in lower Manhattan, she sent him a quick text. She continued to check the phone as the subway rumbled uptown. Grandma kept looking at her disapprovingly, mumbling about kids always being on their devices, but Jessie didn't care. She wanted her dad's name to pop up on the screen.

When they reached their stop, Jessie helped bring Laney's bike over the turnstile and up the subway stairs. They emerged on Lenox Avenue. It was early evening, the sky changing from the bright blue of earlier in the day to a lighter hue, as if a watercolor brush had swooped in and muted the pigment. Jessie, wondering if Mama was still at work, gave her a call.

"Hey, Jessie," said Mama, breathless.

"We're just getting out of the subway right now," Jessie said. "I wanted to see what you were doing."

"Ugh, what a day," Mama said. "I'm missing three of my best workers, and it was going to be me and Manny in the back, but he's sick and couldn't come in."

"Hey!" said another voice through the phone. "You have me, don't you?"

"Is that Auntie Harrigan?" Jessie asked.

Auntie Harrigan's voice came through the speaker again. "I am an *excellent* worker, thank you very much!"

"Auntie Harrigan *did* save me today," Mama admitted.

"And I came up with a fabulous new cookie idea," Auntie Harrigan said.

"I think we'll be here for a couple more hours," Mama told Jessie. "The bakery is a mess, and we still have to take care of the cats."

"We can come by and help, if you want," Jessie said.

"Where?" Laney said. "Is that Mama? Mama, Grandpa got me the best bike ever!"

"Really?" Mama said through the phone.

"Laney is not excited about her bike at all," Jessie said dryly.

"I want to show Mama! Let's go to the bakery!" Laney said.

"Mama, we're heading over. We can help you clean up and take care of the cats so you can come home sooner," Jessie told her while looking at her siblings. They had been listening in on the conversation and nodded.

"That would be wonderful," Mama said.

"Although we *are* doing fine! I'm being very useful!" Auntie Harrigan said.

"See you soon," Jessie said. "Love you."

"Love you," Mama said, and the line disconnected.

"Off to Mama's bakery!" Jessie said, leading the way.

"Yay," Aunt Penny said. "We can see Peaches and Cream again."

They walked north along Lenox to get to Mama's bakery, but as they waited for the light to change at 141st Street, Grandma spoke up.

"We are going back to your apartment," Grandma said. "We are tired."

"You're not coming?" Laney said to Grandpa. "I wanted you to be there when I show Mama my new bike!"

"Are you sure you don't want to come?" Jessie asked. "You can try some of the cookies Mama sells. There's also a cappuccino machine."

"Mmm," Aunt Penny said. "I would love a cappuccino right now."

"We do not drink cappuccino," Grandma said. "Can you give us your keys so we can get inside?"

"Sure," Jessie said, digging her copy of the brownstone keys from her shorts pocket and handing them over.

"Okay, bye," Grandma said. She set off toward the brownstone, Grandpa trailing behind.

"That was weird," Oliver said.

Jessie thought it was weird too, but she didn't have time to think about it because they needed to get to the bakery. They turned on 143rd Street, and the bakery stood out as a warm glow from the twinkle lights illuminating the scalloped yellow-and-white-striped awning. The shadow of a restless cat paced the length of the window. Through the French doors, the handpainted wooden sign was turned to "We're Closed. Come Visit Again!" The door, however, was unlocked, and Jessie opened it and let everyone inside.

Aunt Penny beelined for Peaches and Cream, who were sleeping together in the hamburger bed. Laney and Hyacinth picked them up and cuddled them, then showed Aunt Penny how to clean the litter boxes and feed all the cats, who were circling them, meowing for dinner.

Jessie, Isa, and Oliver opened the door that had two signs: one said "Employees Only" and the other said "No-Cat Zone"! The door opened to a long, narrow hallway that led to the kitchen.

Mama hadn't been joking when she'd said the kitchen was a disaster. Every single mixing bowl was stacked in the sink along with metal whisks, wooden spoons, and plastic spatulas.

"Wow," Oliver said. "This is worse than my bedroom."

Mama, who was peering into the oven to check

on a batch of cookies, stood up and looked over her shoulder.

"Yay!" she said at the sight of her kids.

"Yay!" Auntie Harrigan said at the sight of her nieces and nephew.

"Where are your grandparents?" Mama asked.

"They wanted to go home," Jessie told her. "They were tired."

"Okay," Mama said, and Jessie could see a flash of disappointment streak across her mom's face. Then Aunt Penny walked in.

"Penny!" cried Auntie Harrigan.

They greeted each other with a long hug. Auntie Harrigan turned to the kids.

"I know I just saw you last week, but I swear you all got taller," Auntie Harrigan said to Jessie, Isa, and Oliver as she gave them hugs. She pointed to a tray of cookies cooling on one of the counters. "I made those ginger cookies over there. Give them a taste and let me know what you think. Your mom said we needed a thumbs-up from you before we put them on the menu."

Jessie, Isa, and Oliver didn't have to be asked twice.

They headed for the tray and selected the biggest cookies available.

Oliver was the first to comment. "Mmm," he said, then flashed Auntie Harrigan a thumbs-up.

"I agree," Jessie said after she took a bite and the sugary ginger flavor hit her tongue.

"Awesome," Isa said.

"It's like a party in my mouth," Oliver said.

Auntie Harrigan swiveled to look at Mama. "What do you say?"

"Let's do it," Mama said. "We'll call it Harrigan's Ginger Cookie."

"Yes!" Auntie Harrigan said, pumping her arms in victory.

"Jeez," Aunt Penny said, looking at Auntie Harrigan in mock disgust. "You are really making it hard for me to take over as the Favorite Aunt."

"Ha!" Auntie Harrigan said. "I've worked hard for this position. Plus, I have proximity on my side."

"Maybe I should move," Aunt Penny said, tapping her chin as she thought. "I do love New York City."

"Are you really considering it?" Jessie asked. "That would be amazing."

"Laney and Hyacinth would have cats in your apartment in no time," Isa said.

"You could come to my basketball games," Oliver said. "Auntie Harrigan missed my last two."

Auntie Harrigan sighed. "You know I had those window displays to do. I made it to every single game before that." Auntie Harrigan was a freelance artist and did fun jobs like designing window displays for stores and illustrating menus and signs.

Oliver turned to Aunt Penny. "Are you really thinking of moving here?"

Aunt Penny shook her head. "I love my job in California." Then she changed the subject. "I'm going to tackle those bowls. Don't bother me!" she said with a smile, walking to the industrial sink and tugging on the rubber gloves hanging on the drying rack.

The rest of the group got down to business. Auntie Harrigan turned on the radio, and everyone cleaned until the flour was wiped up, the bowls were sparkling clean, and the steel countertops gleamed. Mama mopped the floor, and then it was time to go home.

Mama flicked off the light and locked the door, and they went back through the hallway and into the bakery.

Hyacinth and Laney sat on the window seat with hair brushes in hand. They were surrounded by a dozen well-fed cats all purring and rubbing against the two girls.

"I think we should take all of them home," Laney said when she saw Mama.

"Okay," Mama said with a smile.

"Papa would not be okay with that," Jessie said. "Imagine the constant smell of cat food."

"Wouldn't it be funny if he came home from Indiana to twelve new cats?" Oliver said.

Jessie checked her phone again to see if Papa had written to her. "Have you heard from him?" she asked Mama.

"No," Mama said. "But I think the signal is really spotty where he is in Indiana. You know how Uncle Sylvester lives in a really rural farming area? There's not much reception."

Just as Mama finished talking, her phone rang. "Hey, it's him!" She tapped something on her screen and held it to her ear. "Hi, honey! We were just talking about you! How's everything going? I figured the reception wasn't great. Here, let me put you on speaker. The kids want to say hi."

Mama pressed a button on her phone, then held it out so everyone could hear.

"Hi, Papa!" Laney said, leaning toward the phone and shouting. "Guess what? Grandpa gave me a bike! A real one! We rode back and forth across the Brooklyn Bridge!"

"That's amazing!" Papa said.

Papa said something else, but there was so much static that no one could understand him.

"Papa, we can't hear you!" Isa said.

There was more static, and they could hear him say "storm" and "bad connection" and "later." Then the line went silent.

"Well, that's a bummer," Mama said. "Sounds like they're getting some weather over there. Maybe he'll call or text later."

After Mama had admired Laney's bike for a satisfactory amount of time, she locked up the bakery and they headed home. The Vanderbeeker kids trailed behind Mama and their aunts. Aunt Penny was telling Mama and Auntie Harrigan how Grandma was on a quest to marry her off.

Mama laughed. "She's relentless!"

Auntie Harrigan glanced at Aunt Penny. "Have you met anyone interesting lately?"

Aunt Penny shrugged. "Work keeps me busy."

"Uh-huh," Auntie Harrigan said.

"Hey, what does that mean?" Aunt Penny asked.

"We think you're afraid of commitment," Mama told her.

The Vanderbeekers perked up. This was getting interesting.

"I'm not afraid of commitment," Aunt Penny protested. "I just want to be certain of success before getting into a relationship. With a pet *or* a person."

"We're never certain of success," Laney said sagely. "We had Franz for a whole year before he said one word to us."

"And now he won't stop barking," Oliver grumbled. "Or drooling. Or stealing food. Or creating general chaos."

"It means he's comfortable with us," Hyacinth said

proudly. "He's not afraid we're going to abandon him anymore."

"Hyacinth wore him down over time," Isa said. "I guess that's how relationships are."

"Did Benny wear *you* down over time?" Laney asked, then turned to Aunt Penny. "Benny Castleman is Isa's boyfriend."

"We're talking about Aunt Penny here," Isa said primly.

"Oh, that guy in the picture on your desk? He's adorable," Aunt Penny said.

"Ick," Oliver said, disgusted.

"I know what you need to do!" Hyacinth said. "You need to adopt Peaches and Cream to get over your fear of commitment."

"I *love* that idea," Mama said.

"I live in California!" Aunt Penny said. "I flew here!"

"You can take cats on the plane," Hyacinth reminded her.

"That's true," Jessie said. "When I went on that plane to Atlanta, I saw someone bring their parrot on the plane. It had a little sign on the cage that said 'emotional support animal.'"

"Yeah, yeah," Aunt Penny said. "But I would like to remind you all that just because I don't have a cat or a relationship, that doesn't mean I'm afraid of commitment!"

"Mmm-hmm," the Vanderbeekers said.

※ ※ ※

When the Vanderbeekers returned home, Laney rolled her new bike into the entryway and leaned it against the wall. She was not going to lock it up outside and risk getting it dirty and rusty. She looked for Grandpa, but he wasn't in the living room, he wasn't in the kitchen, and he wasn't in the bathroom. Then Laney went up the stairs and noticed the door was closed. It was only eight, but her grandparents had already gone to bed.

Laney sighed with disappointment. She didn't like being around Grandma, but she did want to see Grandpa. He always seemed as if he wasn't paying attention, but he'd gotten her the exact kind of bike she wanted.

But it was late, and after a quick dinner of leftovers and then a bath, it was time for bedtime stories. Because they had spent all day with their grandparents, they'd had no time to research Yardsy Loughty, which was another disappointment. But Isa had promised that they would do research first thing the next morning, which was good because tomorrow would be Wednesday and they *really* needed to figure out the trip before Papa's birthday on Saturday. It was supposed to be his present, after all.

In anticipation of story time, Laney set aside a stack of fifteen books, knowing that Mama would have energy for only a couple of them. But as she waited in bed for Mama to arrive, Tuxedo purring contentedly on her pillow, the door opened and Aunt Penny walked in.

"Your mom fell asleep on the couch, so I'm her replacement reader tonight!" Aunt Penny said.

Laney narrowed her eyes. "How are your voices?"

"Voices?" Aunt Penny asked.

"You know, when you read a book. Are your voices good?"

"Um, maybe?"

"I'll just wait for Mama."

Isa stuck her head into the bedroom. "Mama is fast asleep. If you want a bedtime story, Aunt Penny will read to you."

"Why can't you do it?" Laney asked.

"Because I need to practice," Isa said. She blew Laney a kiss. "Love you!"

Aunt Penny picked up a book from Laney's bookshelf. It was called *Drawn Together*, and the cover had a grandfather hugging his grandchild.

"How about this one?" Aunt Penny said.

"No," Laney said. "Only Papa is allowed to read that one to me."

"Why?"

"Because he's really good at it," Laney said. "And I want to save it until he comes home. He gives the best good-night hugs. And he knows just how to tuck me in. Not too tight but nice and cozy."

"Aww, Laney," Aunt Penny said, reaching over to give her a hug. "I remember what it was like when my dad would go away on business trips. I missed him a lot."

Laney blinked. "I don't like it when Papa leaves."

"Okay, we'll save this book until he comes home," she said. "But I do want to read at least one book to you—you can help me with the voices—so can you choose one that's not too hard?"

Laney reached over and picked out *Alma and How*

She Got Her Name and gave it to Aunt Penny. And when her aunt started reading, Laney discovered that Aunt Penny was surprisingly good at voices, although she did mess up a few times by using a high, squeaky voice instead of a slow, low voice. Tired from all the biking and excitement, Laney fell asleep the moment Aunt Penny finished reading and closed the book. She didn't wake up when Hyacinth went to bed, or even when Franz jumped on Laney's bed and kissed her nose. She didn't wake up when a tall stack of books by Oliver's bed fell down and created a terrific clatter, and she didn't wake up at the series of ambulances that went down the street.

But she did wake up later that night, long after everyone was asleep, when the hallway light right outside her bedroom briefly flicked on and cast a beam through her cracked bedroom door and fell right across her face. The light turned off a few seconds later, and Laney sat up and rubbed her eyes. She got up and went down the stairs. She had an idea who had turned on the light, and she crept to the kitchen to confirm her suspicions.

She was right. Grandpa was outside, his motions

slow as he moved through various positions as if he were a dancer. It surprised her how graceful he was. He wasn't the type of person you would imagine moving like a ballet dancer. Laney yearned to step outside and see if she could imitate what he was doing, but she didn't know if Grandpa would be that happy about her interrupting him. She watched for several more minutes, but she was so tired she couldn't keep her eyes open. So she went back upstairs to her warm bed, to Tuxedo curled up on her pillow, and to Hyacinth's light snoring above her.

Laney fell asleep immediately and didn't even notice when, a little while later, her grandfather stepped into her bedroom and tucked the blanket around her, not too tight but nice and cozy.

Wednesday, August 6

Three Days Until Papa's Birthday

Eighteen

Oliver woke up on Wednesday morning with a sense of panic. It was only three days until Papa's birthday and they were no closer to figuring out the mystery of Pop-Pop's trip and how to plan a surprise reenactment. They needed to find Yardsy Loughty *today*. The only problem?

Their grandparents.

Before Oliver went downstairs for breakfast, he stopped by Jessie and Isa's bedroom so he could use their computer. His sisters were still asleep, so Oliver took a seat at Jessie's desk and started doing some internet searches.

They were lucky that Yardsy had such an unusual name, because all Oliver had to do was type in

"Yardsy Loughty" and "New York City" and a dozen results popped up right away. The first one was a *New York Times* article from three years earlier: "Local Boat Builder Offers Classes to Washington Heights Students." Oliver opened the article and read it. Mr. Loughty, who'd been a sanitation worker for forty years, had been an amateur boat builder for several decades and decided to teach local students how to build boats once he retired. He started a nonprofit called Knot Too shabby, where he worked with young people to build full-size traditional rowboats over the course of a school year. There was a photo of Mr. Loughty sanding down the side of a boat with one of the students.

Oliver then looked up the Knot Too Shabby website, which described all the programs they offered. In addition to boat building, the organization led classes in environmental science and sailing. Oliver jotted down the address he found on the bottom of the "Contact Us" page. Then he stood up and walked over to Jessie's bed.

"Jessie, wake up and meet your destiny," Oliver said in his best Darth Vader voice.

Jessie shot up out of bed, and because Oliver did not move fast enough, she cracked her forehead against his.

"Ouch!" they said at the same time.

Across the room, Isa stirred. "What's going on?"

"Oliver, why?" Jessie groaned as she rubbed her red forehead.

"I wanted to show you this," Oliver said. He put the paper in her face.

While Jessie fumbled for her glasses, Isa came over to see the paper.

"What's this address?" Isa asked.

"It's where we're going to find Yardsy Loughty," Oliver said triumphantly.

"Seriously?" Jessie said. "Nice work!"

"Thank you," Oliver said. "Now get out of bed so we can go up to Washington Heights and meet this guy."

❖ ❖ ❖

Mama had already left for the bakery by the time the Vanderbeekers got up. Isa found a note she'd put on the bathroom mirror saying that Manny was out sick again and she was meeting Auntie Harrigan at the bakery so they could get an early start on the day's baking. The kids would be on their own for breakfast and lunch.

Isa read the note, and as she brushed her teeth, she thought about the quickest breakfast that would also satisfy everyone. She was anxious to find Yardsy Loughty and didn't want to let too much time go by before they left for the boat workshop. She could scramble a bunch of eggs and put some of the leftover slices of sourdough bread in the oven to toast. There was fruit she could cut up and bring with them on the subway ride up to Washington Heights as well. Oliver and Laney got particularly grouchy when they were hungry.

She peeked into Hyacinth and Laney's bedroom. Hyacinth was awake and working on her quilt, but she was still in her pajamas. A Laney-sized lump on the bottom bunk confirmed that her youngest sister was still asleep.

"Grandma is downstairs," Hyacinth whispered as she stitched two pieces of fabric together. "I went downstairs at six o'clock to take Franz out and she started asking me questions about my grades, so I told her I was going up to my bedroom to work on Papa's birthday present."

"Oliver found an address where we can find Yardsy Loughty. We're going uptown right after breakfast. Can you wake up Laney and get her changed and her teeth brushed?"

Hyacinth looked at the bed. "I tried to wake her up five minutes ago. She was really tired."

Isa frowned. Laney was usually one of the earlier risers, right after Hyacinth. She sat on Laney's bed and put a hand gently on what she deduced was Laney's back.

"Hey," Isa said. "Time to wake up."

Laney rolled over so Isa could see her face.

"I'm tired today," Laney said, squinting at Isa.

"How did you sleep?" Isa said.

"I woke up in the middle of the night."

"Did you have a bad dream?"

Laney shook her head. "No, I just . . . heard something. And it woke me up."

"I wish I could let you sleep some more, but we've got to get moving to find Pop-Pop's friend. Oliver tracked him down."

"Okay," Laney said, rubbing her eyes.

Isa left the bedroom and made her way down the

stairs. Jessie and Aunt Penny were sitting at the dining room table discussing coral reef biology. As Isa got closer, a new smell filled her nose. Grandma was cooking something on the stove. Grandpa had found a screwdriver kit and was tightening the bolt on a wobbly dining room chair.

"Good morning," Isa said. "What are you doing?"

"What does it look like?" Grandma said. A pot filled with rice and water bubbled slowly on the stove, and Grandma paused to open the spice cabinet to rummage around. "Your mom doesn't even have basic ingredients."

Isa bristled. "Mama is a great cook."

"I had to bring my own ingredients with me." She gestured to the cutting board, where there was a bunch of scallions and a knot of ginger.

"Mama sometimes uses scallions and ginger," Isa said. "Just not every day."

Grandma ignored her. "She had to work again, so I'm making breakfast."

Oliver came down the stairs, raced through the living room, and opened the refrigerator, analyzing the contents.

"What are you doing?" Grandma asked.

Oliver's eyes darted about as if it were a trick question. "Getting something to eat?"

"*I* am making breakfast!"

"If I don't eat something right now my stomach is going to cave in," Oliver said.

"You will wait," Grandma said, walking over to the refrigerator, lightly pushing him out of the way, and closing the door.

The sound of feet thundering down the stairs along with Franz howling gave way to Laney and Hyacinth.

Laney wrinkled her nose. "What's that smell I smell?"

"Grandma is making breakfast," Jessie told them.

"I'm so hungry," Oliver repeated. He looked longingly at the refrigerator.

"You cannot rush this breakfast," Grandma told them. "I was going to start cooking earlier, but I didn't know when you would wake up."

The Vanderbeekers glanced at each other. Isa looked at her watch. Grandma didn't seem to be in any hurry. Jessie nudged Isa and tilted her head toward Grandma, and Isa shook her head slightly. Jessie opened her eyes really wide and angled her head toward Grandma again, and Isa sighed. No one else was going to do it, so it was up to her.

"Grandma," Isa began, "that's so nice of you to make breakfast for us, but we have morning plans to go visit Papa's dad's friend. I was thinking that I would make a quick breakfast for everyone now, and we can have whatever you're making for lunch. Would that be okay?"

Grandma turned and glared at Isa. "We are having this for breakfast."

Isa slumped into a dining room chair. Jessie and Aunt Penny looked at her sympathetically, but there was nothing to do.

So Hyacinth fed a ravenous Franz ("He's such a sloppy eater," Grandma said) and Laney fed the famished Tuxedo and George Washington ("Their food smells disgusting," Grandma said) and Oliver fed the chickens ("I don't know why you're keeping chickens if you're not going to eat them," Grandma said). Even when all the pet feeding was done, breakfast *still* wasn't ready. Oliver looked as if he was going to keel over from hunger.

The Vanderbeekers got utensils out and they sat around the table, watching Grandma slowly cut the green onions into paper-thin slices. She stirred the bubbling pot of white rice and broth and leaned over to breathe in the steam, repeating the process many times. Finally, what seemed like hours later, she turned off the heat.

"Almost done," she announced.

"Thank goodness," Oliver whispered, his head on the table.

Grandpa closed his screwdriver kit and sat on the chair he'd been working on, looking satisfied. Laney sat next to him and joined everyone watching Grandma finish preparations.

Grandma went to the refrigerator, pulled out a package, and unwrapped the pink paper carefully.

"What is that?" Laney asked, her nose wrinkling again.

"I brought it here from the best grocer in Ottenville," Grandma said. "It will go nicely with breakfast. Your mom and uncle loved this when they were growing up."

She put the contents of the package on a platter,

then put the platter in the microwave. The smell of meat filled the apartment.

"That smells like meat," Laney whispered to Isa.

"I think it is meat," Isa whispered back. "Remember, it's okay if you don't want to eat meat, but other people still can if they want to."

Isa stood up and walked to the kitchen.

"Grandma," Isa said, "is that meat in the microwave?"

Grandma nodded just as the microwave dinged. She opened the door and took the platter out.

"Would it be possible," Isa said, "to keep that separate from the rest of breakfast? Hyacinth and Laney don't—"

With one quick motion of her hand, Grandma swept the meat right into the pot.

"—eat meat," Isa finished.

"It is best this way," Grandma said as she brought the pot to the center of the table and put it on a trivet. "The juices get into the soup."

"I don't eat meat," Laney announced.

"Me either," Hyacinth said.

"I do," Oliver said. "Can we start?"

"I'll make you something else," Isa said to her little sisters.

"They should try it," Grandma said. "It's my specialty."

"No, thank you," Hyacinth said.

"Can we have waffles instead?" Laney asked.

Grandma's mouth turned into a line. "You will eat this," she said, taking bowls and spooning soup into them. She set one bowl in front of Laney and one in front of Hyacinth. "This duck is delicious," she assured them.

"Wait," Oliver said. "That's *duck*?"

"Duck like *Make Way for Ducklings*?" Laney said.

"Duck as in the cute birds that live in Central Park?" Hyacinth said.

Grandma looked puzzled. "Don't you ever eat duck?"

Laney and Hyacinth looked down at their bowls, and then they bolted from the table and ran out the back door. A second later, Isa could see them through the window cuddling with Jubilee and Buttercup, two of the larger, friendlier chickens.

Isa saw disappointment flash across Grandma's face before she moved the bowls that were at Laney's and Hyacinth's places to Jessie's and Isa's place mats and put soup in bowls for Oliver, Aunt Penny, and Grandpa.

The Vanderbeekers had never eaten duck before, and Isa wasn't eager to try it. Like Hyacinth, she had loved going to Central Park and watching adorable ducklings follow their parents in the spring.

"Eat," Grandma said, sitting down at the table and gesturing toward the bowls. Grandpa had already started.

Isa looked down into the soup. The pieces of duck were floating at the top of the soup along with cut green onions. Not a fan of green onions either, she used her spoon to scoop them out and put them on top of her napkin. She looked at her siblings, who seemed similarly reluctant about eating duck. Jessie had put a tiny bit of soup—no duck—in her mouth and looked as if she was deciding whether she could swallow it or needed to spit it out. Even ravenous Oliver, who had no qualms about eating hot dogs or hamburgers or turkey chili, was just stirring and stirring his soup, and Isa suspected that he had no plans to actually try it.

Grandma, noticing their tepid reactions, dropped her spoon on the table, stood, and went to the kitchen to begin cleaning up. She left her own soup unfinished.

"Grandma," Isa began, but Grandma just shook her head as she scrubbed the dishes.

"I'll do those, Grandma," Isa said, but Grandma ignored her. Isa turned back to her siblings, and silently the Vanderbeekers poured the contents of the bowls back into the pot and loaded the dishwasher. The dishes in the sink done, Grandma took off her apron, hung it on the nail by the refrigerator, and went up the stairs. A moment later, the Vanderbeekers heard the door to their parents' bedroom close.

Nineteen

Hyacinth felt bad about breakfast, but as she hugged Buttercup to her chest, she knew she couldn't go back inside the brownstone. Her stomach growled, and Buttercup wiggled in her arms. Hyacinth reluctantly let her favorite hen go, and Buttercup scrambled to a worm poking out of the short grass and pecked at it.

"I can't believe Grandma eats duck," Laney repeated for the eighth time. "Duck!"

The back door of the brownstone opened, and Isa stepped out into the yard. She walked over to Laney and Hyacinth and handed them bowls of yogurt with some nuts and dried fruit on top.

"Eat up," Isa said. "We have to get to Washington Heights."

"I'm sorry about breakfast," Hyacinth said.

"I know," Isa said with a sigh. "Grandma seems pretty upset. She went into the bedroom and hasn't come out."

"Did I hurt her feelings?" Laney asked.

"I think we all did," Isa said. "Come on, eat your yogurt. We should get going."

Hyacinth and Laney ate the yogurt. It tasted good the way Isa made it, with lots of nuts and fruit and a little drizzle of honey. And while Hyacinth ate, she wondered if Mama really did love that duck and rice soup. It was strange, learning all these new things about her parents.

Finished with their breakfast, Hyacinth and Laney went inside to wash their bowls. Oliver and Jessie were sitting on the couch, waiting for them.

"Where's Aunt Penny?" Hyacinth asked.

"Mr. Beiderman and Orlando stopped by to see if anyone wanted to go for a run," Oliver said. "Aunt Penny said she wanted some exercise and would meet us back here for lunch."

"I didn't know Aunt Penny liked to run," Laney said.

"We don't know a lot about the adults in our lives," Hyacinth said. "They're all mysteries."

"Are we ready to go?" Isa asked, stuffing a bag of trail mix into her backpack. She opened the door, and after everyone had followed her outside, she closed it softly behind them so as not to disturb Grandma and Grandpa.

"I still feel bad about breakfast," Hyacinth said to Isa as they walked to the number 1 subway station on 145th Street.

"I know," Isa said. "We'll talk to her when we get back."

"Let's be honest," Oliver said. "She came here completely unannounced and has spent the majority of her time with us criticizing or complaining. It hasn't exactly been fun."

"I'm *so* glad Papa is coming home tomorrow," Laney said. "I can't wait to hug him."

They went down the steps into the subway station and swiped their cards through the turnstiles. They listened to a man playing the saxophone and dug some spare change out of pockets and backpacks, then dropped the coins into the man's case. A few minutes later, the subway roared into the station, the big red circle with a block white "1" in the middle on the front.

They needed to ride the train to Dyckman Street, which was a quick ten-minute trip north. When the train emerged on an elevated track, the Vanderbeekers got off the subway and enjoyed the novelty of disembarking outside. Tall trees surrounded the station, and it felt as if they had entered a different world. They went down the metal stairs to the street and walked toward the East River. There was a rocky park filled with huge trees on the right and a wide street to the left. They crossed the street and went north on Tenth Avenue. Right away they saw a red brick school, and next to the school was a dirt path with a sign and a big garden gnome.

"This is it," Isa said.

Hyacinth loved the peacefulness of the path. On either side, zinnias and dahlias burst open like miniature suns, and flowering vines wrapped around stakes. Large trees stretched skyward on either side, their leaves dappling the sunlight onto the ground and making tiny shards of mica from the path sparkle.

The Vanderbeekers emerged on a joyous scene: A dozen kids in light blue T-shirts that said "Knot Too Shabby Summer Camp" were clustered around the skeleton of a boat propped upside down on a wooden frame.

When the Vanderbeekers appeared, one of the campers saw them and waved. "Want to see our boat?" she asked.

The Vanderbeekers nodded, and the camper gestured them over.

"We're trying to get this done by next month so we can put it in the water before school starts again!" the girl said. "I'm Selah, by the way. Why do you have red and green dots all over you?" she said, looking at Laney and Oliver.

"Long story," Oliver said.

The Vanderbeekers introduced themselves, and

then all the kids wearing the Knot Too Shabby shirts introduced themselves, and told the Vanderbeekers how they were building a boat, which seemed like a very long and complicated process. Hyacinth could only make out parts of what they were saying, words like "keel" and "laminating boards" and "clamps" and "bevel" and "marine lumber."

A minute later, a man emerged from the big open garage and approached them. He also wore a Knot Too Shabby T-shirt, but his was yellow.

"What's going on here?" he said, his voice booming.

The Vanderbeekers turned to look at him, and the man instantly went still.

"I know you," he said after a few moments of silence.

"We know you too," Laney said.

"We know *of* you, she means," Jessie clarified.

"That is, if you're the person we're actually looking for," Isa said.

"I think you are the person we're looking for," Oliver said.

"I think you're Yardsy Loughty," Laney announced.

He nodded, his eyes very shiny and bright. "And I think you are the Vanderbeekers."

Laney looked at Yardsy, examining his features. He wasn't as tall as Papa, and he had really wide shoulders like Orlando. He was completely bald, but his eyebrows were very bushy, nearly covering his eyes, and when he smiled, you could look right into them and see a lot of love.

He walked over and looked at Isa and Jessie. "You two have your grandfather's eyes."

He looked at Oliver. "You have your grandfather's hair."

He looked at Hyacinth. "You have your grandfather's nose."

And he looked at Laney. "You, I think, have your grandfather's spirit."

"You were Pop-Pop's best friend," Laney told him. "And that's why *we're* going to be really good friends."

Yardsy burst into laughter. "Oh boy, you definitely remind me of your grandfather. He made me laugh like no one else. Now tell me how you found me."

"We found out about you from Jamal," Isa told

him at the same time Oliver said, "We found this letter that Pop-Pop wrote to our dad," and Laney said, "We came on a subway and got off at a really tall subway station," and Jessie said, "We looked up your name on the internet." Hyacinth wasn't a fan of talking to people she didn't know very well, so she said nothing.

Yardsy laughed again. "I need to sit down for this. Come with me into the workshop. I want to hear the whole story." Yardsy told his campers to keep up the good work and to put some more clamps on the boat, then led the Vanderbeekers to the garage. They stepped inside the workshop, and Laney breathed in the smell of trees and sawdust. There were six more boats in various states of being built.

"I'm working with five groups of middle schoolers this summer," Yardsy told them as he took a seat on an upside-down crate. "And one of the boats is my personal project."

Laney looked at the beautiful wood, thinking about the trees it came from and how it was now going to be something that allowed people to float on the water. It filled her with awe.

"Where did this wood come from?" Laney asked.

"We get donations from lumberyards and some of the bigger boat-making companies," Yardsy said. "We've got some ash, some cedar, and a little bit of oak."

"I want to learn how to build a boat," Laney said. "It looks cool."

"And I would love to help you make one," Yardsy said. "I am glad you found me. Life is a funny thing. I've been thinking about your grandfather a lot these days. He keeps appearing in my mind in the strangest places. Last week, I was on the water early Sunday morning, rowing on the perfect quiet of the East River, and I remembered how he would bring me the best croissant from a bakery near his apartment."

"That's Castleman's Bakery!" Oliver said. "We go there all the time."

"We're trying to learn more about him," Laney told Yardsy. "We found a letter he wrote to our dad right before graduation. He said he was taking Papa on a trip. And we're trying to figure out where they were going."

"He said he wanted to go somewhere called Whalers Cove," Oliver said.

"Ah, I remember your grandfather getting ready

for that. He was so excited. He rarely took time off from work, and I was surprised that he wanted to make such a long trip. They were going to leave for a full month."

"A month at Whalers Cove?" Isa asked.

"And other places," Yardsy said. "It was a road trip, you know."

"A road trip!" the Vanderbeekers all exclaimed at once.

"That makes so much sense now!" Isa said. "Ludwig *van* Beethoven. Ludwig is the name of the van they were going to use, wasn't it?"

Yardsy smiled. "Yes."

"Do you know what route he wanted to take?" Jessie asked.

"I know he had a whole itinerary written out," Yardsy said. "He worked on it during our lunch breaks. It was so long ago, I can't remember where exactly he wanted to go. He had a very detailed map. If your dad kept some of his things, the map might be there."

"We could look through that stuff from Grandpa's old suitcase again," Oliver said.

"I wonder what happened to that van," Yardsy said. "It was a white van he was borrowing from a friend."

"So Pop-Pop didn't name it?" Isa asked.

"I don't think so," Yardsy said. "I think it came with the name. The owner was a mechanic, so the van worked like a dream. It could easily have done a cross-country trip."

"Cross-country?" Jessie asked. "Are you saying that Whalers Cove is on the West Coast?"

"California," Yardsy confirmed. "I don't remember where exactly."

"I tried to find it in California," Jessie told him. "But I couldn't find anything linked to a military base. That's where Pop-Pop's dad was stationed during the war."

Yardsy thought for a moment, then shook his head. "I can't remember exactly what part of California. It's a big state, so I can imagine it would be hard to find."

"You should come to Papa's birthday party this Saturday at three o'clock," Laney said. "He's turning forty."

Yardsy smiled. "Forty. Wow. I haven't seen Derek for years. I would love to come and wish him a happy birthday."

Isa wrote the location on a piece of paper, and Yardsy gave them his business card with his cell phone number scrawled on it.

"Call me if you need anything," Yardsy said. Then he looked at Laney. "I expect to hear from you when you're ready to build a boat."

"Can we do it tomorrow?" she asked.

Yardsy laughed. "Building a boat takes a long time. Those kids out there? They started that boat back in June!"

"Wow!" Laney said. "That is a long time."

"It's slow, careful work," Yardsy said. "You can't rush it."

"Maybe you can tell us stories about Pop-Pop while we work on it," Laney suggested.

"I think that's a fine idea."

Outside, the shouts and laughter of the summer camp kids drifted into the workshop and mingled with the fresh sawdust. Laney tucked the memory of that moment into her heart while Yardsy said, "I'll tell you one story about him, and then I've got to get back to work. We were finishing our last garbage pickup one morning, and in the rearview mirror your grandfather saw a woman running behind us. Her hair was in curlers and she was wearing slippers and pajamas. Now, before you think this story makes me look bad and makes your grandfather look like a hero, keep in mind that I was hungry and tired and it was a hot summer day.

"The truth is, I did not want to stop for her. But your grandpa didn't listen to me, and he screeched to a halt and jumped out of the truck. The woman was frantic. She thought she had accidentally thrown away a ring that belonged to her great-grandma when she was cooking the previous night. I told her it would be impossible to look for a tiny ring in a truck full of garbage."

"That doesn't sound very helpful of you," Laney said.

"I told you this story doesn't make me look that good. Remember, I was tired, I was hungry, and I smelled. But the woman said, 'I'm ninety-nine percent sure.' I was about to say, 'Too bad,' but your grandfather told her that we had to bring the truck to the disposal area and dump out the contents and she could go through it. But first she needed to put on some different clothes because going through garbage could be dangerous.

"She ran home and was back in five minutes in jeans and big leather hiking boots. She got into the garbage truck, hair still in curlers, and rode with us to the disposal site. We dumped the load in this one area. I was all ready to say see ya later, but your grandfather insisted that we help her look. So we put on hard hats, gloves, protective glasses, and vests and got to work."

"I'm glad you helped her," Hyacinth told him.

"Me too. You wouldn't imagine the types of things people throw out! Your grandfather was excellent at finding things. Once he found a garden gnome right in the middle of a trash pile. I liked it so much that I washed it off and brought it home. Now it's on the path here, right by the sign. You saw it, right?"

The Vanderbeekers nodded.

"I love that gnome," Laney told him. "Does he have a name?"

"His name is Gnome."

"I'm going to give him a better name," Laney said. "Jerome the Gnome. Gnome of the City Shire. Vincent. Which one do you like?"

"Anyway," Yardsy continued, "it took us two hours to find the bag that the woman had discarded. Thank goodness she put her garbage in a distinctive grocery bag from Fairway. We opened up the bag and searched carefully. Your father found the ring in a bunch of garlic and ginger peels. The woman thanked us a hundred times and insisted on having us over for dinner the next night. Your Pop-Pop declined—he liked to be home in the evenings so he could be with your father, who was probably around seven at the time—but it looked to me like this lady was a great cook based on what we found in her garbage, so I said yes. I went the next evening and realized I really liked her. To my surprise, she liked me too."

"Even though you were sort of mean about letting her look through the garbage?" Oliver asked.

"Yup. A year later, we ended up getting married. We just celebrated our thirty-second wedding anniversary."

"Wow!" the Vanderbeekers said.

"So Pop-Pop was responsible for your marriage," Isa said.

"He sure was," Yardsy said. "And he didn't just do that kind of stuff with me. He did those types of things all the time. I look forward to telling you more stories when you come and build that boat."

The sounds from the campers were getting louder, so Yardsy said, "I've got to make sure those kids are doing okay. When I come on Saturday for the party, we can set up times for you to come by."

"We would love that," Isa said. "Thank you."

The Vanderbeekers said goodbye to Yardsy and the campers and went back down the path to the sidewalk, pausing to look at the garden gnome by the Knot Too Shabby sign.

"I can't believe Pop-Pop pulled this out of the garbage," Oliver said, touching the gnome's funny, faded hat. "And now it's here, decades later."

"Now we know that Whalers Cove is in California," Jessie said. "We can narrow down the search this afternoon."

"I wonder if that van is still out there somewhere," Laney said.

"Probably not," Oliver said. "It's been almost two decades since that trip was planned."

Laney patted the gnome on the head ("Goodbye, Vincent!" she said), and the Vanderbeekers made their way back to the subway station, up the stairs, and back onto the 1 train, this time going downtown to Harlem.

"I forgot for a while," Laney said when they got off at 145th Street and emerged onto the sidewalk.

"Forgot what?" Isa asked.

"I forgot that Grandma is at home waiting for us."

And just like that, the Vanderbeekers' good mood vanished.

Twenty

When the Vanderbeekers stepped inside the brownstone, Franz howled in delight at being reunited with Hyacinth, Paganini jumped in erratic circles in the hallway while Tuxedo chased after him, and George Washington leaped onto the side table by the door and slid on the mail gathered there, knocking the stack of envelopes and catalogs to the floor.

Aunt Penny, Mr. Beiderman, and Orlando were in the kitchen making lunch, but Grandma and Grandpa were nowhere to be found.

"Hey," Jessie said after plucking George Washington off the table and putting the mail back. "We're home."

"How was your morning?" Aunt Penny called from the kitchen. "I mean, after breakfast, that is."

"It was so great," Hyacinth told her. "We tracked down one of Pop-Pop's best friends. They worked together at the sanitation department!"

"And now he teaches kids how to build boats," Laney said. "And he's going to teach us how to build our own boat!"

"Wow!" Orlando said. "I've always wanted to do that."

"Maybe we can find one day a week to go uptown together after school," suggested Jessie.

While Aunt Penny made grilled cheese sandwiches and Mr. Beiderman tossed a giant salad, Jessie told Orlando what had happened that morning with her grandma.

"I don't know what her problem is," Jessie told him in hushed tones as she rustled through the utensil drawer for forks. "She's so critical. We can never be enough for her."

"I wonder if something happened to your grandma when she was growing up that made her the way she is," Orlando said. "Sometimes really critical people are most critical about themselves."

Jessie thought about what Orlando said. "I guess that makes sense, but it doesn't make it any easier to be around her."

"I get that," Orlando said.

"Do you know where she is?" Jessie asked.

Orlando shook his head. "I haven't seen her. Maybe she's in the bedroom? Your grandfather is outside."

Jessie stood up and looked out the back window. Laney was already outside with him, riding her bike around the small yard while the chickens squawked and raced to get out of her way. Grandpa was fixing loose slats on the chicken coop.

"Now, Grandpa, he's also a mystery," Jessie said. "He doesn't talk much, but it's like he's watching and observing everyone so carefully. And he keeps on fixing things around the brownstone."

"Sounds like someone else we know," Orlando said, tilting his head toward the living room, where Hyacinth was sitting on the couch with Franz as she worked on her quilt square.

"Hey," Oliver said, nudging Jessie. "We should go do research about Whalers Cove now."

"Yeah," Jessie said, then glanced toward the stairs. "But I also feel like we should do something with Grandma and Grandpa first, since we left them alone this morning."

Oliver shrugged. "I guess. But we really do need to find out more about that road trip. His birthday is on Saturday."

"We'll do our research after we spend some time with them," Jessie said before walking to the kitchen and standing next to Mr. Beiderman, who was shaking up the salad dressing. "Aunt Penny, do you know of anything Grandma would want to do today?"

"Well," Aunt Penny said, neatly flipping a grilled cheese sandwich in a frying pan to reveal a beautifully browned piece of bread, "she loves gardening. You remember her beautiful garden back at her house, don't you?"

"I guess I didn't really notice it the last time we were there," Jessie said. "Maybe I would appreciate it more now, since we have a garden of our own."

"We should take Grandma to the New York Botanical Garden," Isa suggested.

"Ugh, no," Oliver said. "We're already going on Saturday for Papa's birthday. It's so boring there."

"That's an excellent idea," Mr. Beiderman said, ignoring Oliver. "I might tag along. I haven't been there in a few months. Maybe Miss Josie will want to go as well."

Miss Josie used to work at the New York Botanical Garden. In fact, it was where she met her husband, Mr. Jeet.

"It would take up the rest of the afternoon," Oliver groaned.

"We don't have to stay that long," Jessie said. "And it would be a way to care for Grandma."

"Okay," Oliver grumbled. Then he said quietly to Jessie, "I'm just getting worried that we haven't found Whalers Cove yet."

"We'll spend all evening doing research," Jessie promised. She climbed the stairs and went down the hallway to knock on her parents' door.

"Who is it?" Grandma asked.

"Jessie."

Grandma opened the door. Her expression was carefully blank.

"Aunt Penny and Mr. Beiderman are almost done making lunch," Jessie told her. "After we eat, we thought you might want to go to the New York Botanical Garden."

Grandma nodded, but her expression remained neutral. "Okay."

Jessie smiled at her and they both went downstairs to find everyone grabbing seats and helping themselves to salad and the giant mountain of grilled cheese sandwiches. Lunch was fast, and Jessie could tell that Aunt Penny was once again startled at how quickly the food disappeared.

"I don't know how your mother does it," Aunt Penny said, shaking her head.

"She's amazing," Laney said.

Jessie noticed that Grandma didn't say anything.

Lunch was consumed within a few minutes, and then the Vanderbeekers cleaned quickly so they could get going. Miss Josie did want to go with them, so it was a quite a big group heading to the Metro North station on 125th Street and Park Avenue. It was a beautiful day, though, and everyone was happy to walk.

Grandma didn't seem to be in the mood to talk, but everyone else was chatting and laughing, even Hyacinth and Grandpa. Orlando and Miss Josie peppered Aunt Penny with questions about her work at the Monterey Bay Aquarium, while Oliver told Grandpa and Grandma about training with the high school basketball team and Jessie listened in, ready to put a positive spin on it if Grandma began questioning his purpose in life.

Jessie suppressed a yawn as they arrived at the train station. It sure was exhausting keeping up with everything.

❀ ❀ ❀

Hyacinth waited with the others as Isa and Aunt Penny went to the ticket counter and purchased eleven round-trip tickets to the New York Botanical Garden. It was a quick ride, only about twenty minutes, and when they got off, they were right across the street from the entrance. Grandma remained pretty quiet during the trip, and even though Hyacinth could sense that she was still upset from the morning, there was some relief that she wasn't nagging them.

They first went to the orchid show in the conservatory. As they stepped into the humid building, orchids in all shapes and sizes surrounded them in a riot of color. Hyacinth was stunned by the beauty. Even though she had been to the orchid show each year for the past three years, the exhibits were always slightly different and never failed to fill her with joy. Just looking at the flowers made her want to create something. Meanwhile, Jessie and Orlando examined the orchids and read every single informational placard.

" 'Orchidaceae is a member of Asparagales, an order of monocotyledonous flowering plants that also includes the asparagus and iris families,' " Orlando read out loud.

"I had no idea that they're in the same family as asparagus," Jessie said. "Fascinating."

"Who knew?" Orlando said, as they moved on to the next placard.

Oliver, who wasn't a fan of the botanical garden—too boring—walked with Mr. Beiderman and Aunt Penny. While Mr. B chatted with Aunt Penny about his new hobby—making soap sculptures—Oliver entertained himself by making recommendations to Mr. B about what he should make next. So far Oliver had suggested a porcupine and a replica of Michelangelo's David sculpture.

Laney was holding hands with Miss Josie, and their heads were close together as they chatted about something. Grandma and Grandpa walked together, their fingers intertwined.

After they had gone through the entire exhibit, they exited into the open garden. Hyacinth breathed in the summer air, which felt good in her lungs after the humid exhibit. Miss Josie had noticed that Grandma was particularly interested in the Cattleya orchid at the show, a pretty, speckled orchid with delicate petals. They were sold in the gift shop, Miss Josie said, and she thought Grandma might want to take a look.

They headed toward the gift shop, which was busy with lots of people roaming around. Oliver, Orlando, Jessie, Mr. Beiderman, Aunt Penny, and Grandpa peeked inside the busy store then said they would wait outside. But Hyacinth and Laney wanted to see the orchids, so Isa agreed to bring them in. Miss

Josie led Grandma to the room where the live orchids were kept while Isa, Hyacinth, and Laney followed behind.

It took a while for them to make their way to the orchid area. People clustered around the tables, examining the hundreds of orchids for sale. Hyacinth was wondering if she had enough pocket money to get an orchid of her own when she saw a tall man bump into Grandma, causing her to stumble into a table holding a display of silk scarves.

"Excuse me," Grandma murmured.

The man looked down at her, and Hyacinth did not like the look on his face. His eyes were squinty and his lips were twisted into a mean smirk.

"*Accuse* you?" the man said.

Grandma just stood there, a polite smile on her lips. "Excuse me, please."

"*Accuse* you please?"

Miss Josie, who had turned around in time to witness the exchange, marched back to Grandma and stood in front of her like a shield. "She said 'Excuse me," Miss Josie said icily. "Now leave her alone."

"Yeah," Laney called from a few yards away. "*You* bumped into *her. You* should be saying sorry."

Hyacinth wanted to add something, to tell him that he was mean and shouldn't talk to people like that, but she couldn't get her mouth to say anything.

The man shook his head and pointed at Grandma. "I can't understand a word she's saying. If you live here, you could speak the language."

Miss Josie stood up straighter. "She speaks beautifully. Which is more than I can say about the words coming out of *your* mouth."

People were gathering around them at this point, and Hyacinth noticed that many of them were looking at the man in disapproval.

"I just want to live in a country where I understand what people are saying," he muttered as he walked away. "Is that so wrong?"

At his departure, customers went back to minding their business, and space opened enough for Hyacinth and her sisters to get to Grandma.

"Are you okay?" Isa asked her.

"Of course," Grandma said. "It is not a big deal."

"It's a shame people are so ignorant," Miss Josie told her. "Don't spend one second thinking about that guy."

Grandma looked at Miss Josie. "Let's go home," she said.

Twenty-One

When they returned from the New York Botanical Garden, Mr. Beiderman, Miss Josie, and Orlando went upstairs to their apartments and Grandma continued to pretend that nothing had happened. When Isa tried to bring up the scene in the gift shop, Grandma just waved her hand in the air like it didn't matter.

But Isa knew that it did matter—it bothered her, and she wasn't even involved!—and she wasn't sure why Grandma acted like it was no big deal. It made Isa wonder if things like that happened often to Grandma and Grandpa. It reminded her that her grandparents had a whole story she knew nothing about.

Shortly after they arrived home, while Jessie went upstairs to research Whalers Cove in California, Isa went into the basement to practice her violin. She began slowly with scales and arpeggios, being careful with each note to make sure it rang clearly and was perfectly in tune. Next she worked on a new etude that Mr. Van Hooten had assigned, struggling with the continuous barrage of double stops, or places where she had to play on two strings at the same time.

"You are out of tune," her grandma said from behind her.

Isa, startled that someone was down in the basement without her knowing, jumped and knocked her bow against the music stand.

"Be careful with your bow!" Grandma exclaimed. "Very expensive."

"You startled me," Isa said.

"Play it again, in tune," Grandma said.

Isa played it again, and Grandma shook her head. "You need to focus."

"Okay, Grandma," Isa said, and she tried it again.

"No, no," Grandma said to her. "It's not right."

And so it went for the next thirty minutes, Isa playing and Grandma correcting her, until Jessie stuck her head downstairs and said that Aunt Penny needed Grandma's help with something.

Isa sighed with relief at Grandma's departure. She got back to work, focusing on her double stops without Grandma's endless criticism, then went on to play her orchestral music and solo piece. Above her, she could hear the steady beats of family life: the clangs in the kitchen and the roll of Laney's bike wheels and the thump of Oliver's basketball (before Grandma told him to stop playing ball in the apartment). And then, as Isa got wrapped inside the music, the sounds faded into the background until Jessie called her upstairs for dinner.

Mama was working late at the bakery again, so Aunt Penny cooked. The spicy smells of garlic and ginger and cilantro filled Isa's nose.

"Aunt Penny made Indian food for dinner!" Laney told Isa.

"She even made naan," Oliver said.

"That's my favorite bread in the world," Laney reported.

"I know," Isa said as she washed her hands and joined the family at the table. "This looks absolutely delicious. Thanks, Aunt Penny." She glanced at Grandma and wondered if she liked Indian food.

Grandma seemed particularly grouchy at dinner, and she was relentless with her criticism during the meal. She thought the dishes that Aunt Penny made were too spicy, even though spice-sensitive Laney happily ate all of it. She said that Isa needed to focus more during violin practice, and that Oliver should be doing math every day—summer did not mean taking a break from math. Jessie needed to get her hair cut, and why did she always wear such baggy clothes? Hyacinth needed to stop mumbling—who could understand a word she was saying? Laney should keep her bedroom cleaner—it was like a pigsty in there.

"Actually," Laney said, "pigs are very clean. They *never* go to the bathroom near their living area—"

Grandma shushed her. "Don't talk about such things at dinner."

When dinner was finally over, Isa and her siblings cleaned up the kitchen while Grandma sat on a stool and pointed at parts of the kitchen that were dirty. When Isa told her that they had everything under control and suggested that Grandma and Grandpa should feel free to get some rest, she was surprised when her grandparents actually agreed and went upstairs. Aunt Penny and the Vanderbeekers relaxed at their departure.

"Dinner was great," Isa told her aunt as they cleaned up.

"Even though it was spicy enough to light your tongue on fire?" Aunt Penny said with a grin, echoing Grandma's comments.

"Grandma's been worse since the botanical garden," Jessie noted.

"Maybe she's upset by what happened in the store," Hyacinth said.

"It sounded terrible," Aunt Penny said. "It reminded me of the things that happened to my parents when we were growing up. A lot of people made fun of their accents or told them to go back where they came from. And if it happened to my parents, it definitely happened to your grandparents."

"It's weird how she seemed to completely forget about it," Isa said.

"I don't think she forgot about it," Aunt Penny said. "I think she's learned how to live with it."

"That's really sad," Laney said. "I wouldn't want people saying stuff like that to me all the time."

"Me either," Aunt Penny said, giving Laney a hug, then glancing at the time. "You know what? I think I'm going to walk over to your mom's bakery to see if she needs help cleaning up."

Laney and Hyacinth looked at her with glee.

"You totally want to visit Peaches and Cream!" Laney said.

Aunt Penny grinned.

"You should—" Laney began.

"I'm not adopting them," Aunt Penny interrupted. "Remember? I live across the country. I have a busy life."

"Uh-huh," Laney and Hyacinth said.

Aunt Penny rolled her eyes, then put her phone in the back pocket of her jeans and headed out the door.

The brownstone was quiet after she left, and the Vanderbeekers immediately felt the weight of the day press down on them.

"I miss Papa," Laney said.

"Let's call him," Isa said. She took out her phone, called his number, and put it on speaker. It rang six times before disconnecting. "That's weird," Isa said. "Let me try again." But the second try yielded the same results.

"He's probably not getting good reception," Jessie said. "At least he's coming home tomorrow."

"I can't wait to see him," Hyacinth and Laney said at the same time.

"Speaking of Papa," Oliver said, "we have to find Whalers Cove. His birthday is only three days away."

"I did some research this afternoon but didn't see anything," Jessie said. "But it reminded me that we should look through the box of things that belonged to Pop-Pop. Maybe the itinerary is in there."

The Vanderbeekers went upstairs to Isa and Jessie's bedroom, where they could get to work. Jessie got on the computer while Isa pulled up the internet browser on her phone. Laney and Hyacinth started paging through the books they had checked out from the library. Oliver sifted through the box of Pop-Pop's things, which they had moved from Mama and Papa's bedroom when their grandparents had arrived. With the exception of a couple of fun photograph albums from when Papa was a boy and a few boring legal documents, there was nothing of interest among Pop-Pop's belongings. Two hours later, they had made no progress.

They could not find Whalers Cove anywhere.

✧ ✧ ✧

Laney was so exhausted from the day that she fell asleep instantly. But just as she had the previous two nights, she woke to the sound of someone walking down the stairs. This time she wasn't scared because she knew it was Grandpa heading to the backyard. She waited until she could hear the click of the back door closing, then got out of bed and went down the stairs. She passed Mama and Aunt Penny sleeping in the living room and crept to her spot by the back window.

Once again, Grandpa was doing his mysterious movements, and Laney watched him glide back and forth through the grass, his arms making big circles in the space around him. The gestures were so beautiful and welcoming that Laney found herself opening the back door and stepping out into the damp night.

Grandpa noticed her right away, but he just smiled at her and kept going. Laney made her way to the grass and began imitating him. She knew her movements didn't look like his—he moved as if he were dancing underwater—but it felt good to be out in the stillness of the night. She loved feeling the cool breeze against her cheek and the dewy grass under her feet.

Grandpa had always been a mystery. She didn't understand his quiet ways, yet being outside with him and connecting through movement made her feel closer to him. Laney wasn't sure how long they were out there, but when Grandpa was done, he turned to her and gave her an unexpected hug. She took his hand and they went back inside, tiptoed through the living room, and climbed the stairs. Grandpa waved as he stepped into Mama and Papa's bedroom while Laney went to her bedroom. Even though it was so late, she could not sleep. She tried all the tricks Papa had taught her. She tried making her breaths nice and even, petting Tuxedo's forehead, and visualizing the best moment of her week so far: riding over the Brooklyn Bridge on her new bike with Grandpa.

Still unable to fall asleep, Laney turned in her bed and caught a glimpse of the big book they had checked out from the library two days earlier. She flipped on the night-light, heaved the huge book into her bed, and began to read.

THURSDAY, AUGUST 7

Two Days Until Papa's Birthday

Twenty-Two

Oliver was having a great dream. He was the starting point guard for his middle school basketball team, playing alongside Angie, Jimmy L, Orlando, and . . . Laney? Never mind. He ran out onto the court as the announcer called his name, a packed stadium cheering for him. It sounded as if people were stamping their feet in excitement. He looked for his teammates, and Laney was yelling something at him.

"What?" Oliver said over the noise.

"Whalers Cove!"

And with that, his fantastic dream vanished, and Oliver bolted up in bed.

Laney was tugging at his blanket, saying, "I found it! I found Whalers Cove!"

Jessie, Isa, and Hyacinth must have heard the commotion, because they were standing in the doorway of his tiny room, saying, "Really? Whalers Cove? How? Where?"

More footsteps came from the hall, and Aunt Penny, who had just come out of the upstairs bathroom, appeared in the doorway behind his sisters. "Are you talking about the Whalers Cove in California?"

Laney turned to look at Aunt Penny. "Yes, I found it! It's in—"

"Point Lobos," Laney and Aunt Penny said at the same time.

Laney looked at Aunt Penny and said, "How did you know where it was?" while Aunt Penny said, "I love Whalers Cove! It's so close to where I live!"

Then all five Vanderbeekers said, "You live by Whalers Cove?" at the same time Aunt Penny said, "Why you are interested in Whalers Cove?"

There was a pause as everyone waited for someone else to start talking, and when no one did, Laney said, "We've been trying to find Whalers Cove *forever.* We found a letter that Pop-Pop wrote to Papa the day before he died saying that he wanted to take Papa there."

"Let me show you the letter," Isa said, dashing into her bedroom and returning a few seconds later. She handed it to Aunt Penny, and the Vanderbeekers watched as Aunt Penny read it.

"Wow," Aunt Penny said after she had read it twice. "That is an incredible letter."

"We've been trying to find Whalers Cove all week," Laney told her. "And last night I couldn't sleep, so I started reading my book about the important sites of World War Two, and then I *found* it: Whalers Cove in Point Lobos, California."

Her siblings and Aunt Penny looked at Laney, amazed.

"Whalers Cove is one of my favorite places to take a walk," Aunt Penny said. "There's an old fishing cabin there that was converted to headquarters for secret military operations during World War Two."

"And there were a bunch of people who lived there during the war and made a radar station so they would know if objects were coming toward them from far away," Laney said.

"And the army used it to train solders of the 543rd Amphibious Brigade in the use of landing craft," Aunt Penny said.

"And the army would do drills where they would land boats on the beach and then run up to the meadow," Laney finished.

Isa, Jessie, Oliver, and Hyacinth just stared at Aunt Penny and Laney.

"What? I like history, okay?" Aunt Penny said.

"That library book has a *lot* of information in it," Laney said.

"Are you telling me," Oliver said to Aunt Penny, "that you knew about Whalers Cove all this time?"

Aunt Penny nodded. "I wish I had known you were looking for it!"

"We want to re-create that trip for Papa," Isa told her. "But we didn't know where Whalers Cove was. The letter didn't say, and we couldn't find information on the internet."

"Books rule!" crowed Laney.

"I know about Whalers Cove, but I don't know about anything else in that letter," Aunt Penny said. "Like who is Ludwig? That's a terrible name."

"We found that out from Yardsy," Oliver told her. Then he explained the van and lost itinerary.

"What a shame," Aunt Penny said. "But at least you know where Whalers Cove is. And if you go, you can stay with me!"

"That would be awesome," Isa told her.

"But we really want to give him the *whole* experience," Oliver said. "He's turning forty on Saturday, and last year we got Mama a bakery for her fortieth birthday, so . . ."

"Well," Aunt Penny said reasonably, "I think your dad would be happy with a trip to Whalers Cove even if you don't have any of the other locations. I think that would be very special."

Isa and Jessie said, "You're right," but Oliver was unconvinced.

Another set of footsteps came down the hall, and Mama appeared in the crowded doorway.

"Kids," she said, her face creased in worry, "there was a big tornado last night in Indiana."

The Vanderbeekers froze, afraid to hear Mama's next words.

"Papa and Uncle Sylvester and the whole family are

fine," Mama said quickly, and Oliver's heart resumed beating. "But the tornado created a lot of destruction in the area."

"He's still coming back today, right?" Laney asked, her fingers pulling at the sleeves of her pajamas.

"He is not," Mama said. "The airport he was leaving from had a lot of damage, and the other local airports are pretty small, so there are no available seats on planes to New York City today."

"So he's coming back tomorrow?" Hyacinth asked.

"The earliest flight he could get is next Tuesday."

"*Next Tuesday?*" the Vanderbeekers said in unison.

"But his birthday is this Saturday!" Laney said.

"What about his party?" Oliver said.

Mama shook her head. "I'm sorry. We have to cancel the party."

✵ ✵ ✵

Downstairs, gathered in the living room, the Vanderbeekers considered whether to simply reschedule the party for the following Saturday, but Mama said they should wait to set a new date just in case Papa couldn't get home next Tuesday.

"Do you mean he might be gone *longer*?" Laney said, distraught.

"We just don't know," Mama said as she headed out the door. "We'll have to see."

"This stinks," Jessie said, slumping down on the couch.

Grandma, who was sitting at the dining room table and trying to shoo Tuxedo off without actually touching her, paused to glare at Jessie. "Language, Jessie. And sit up straight. Your posture is terrible."

Jessie ignored her.

"We need to contact everyone on the guest list," Isa said.

So the Vanderbeekers retreated again to Isa and Jessie's bedroom and spent the next couple of hours calling and emailing everyone they had invited. Thankfully, the handful of people traveling by airplane had purchased travel insurance, so they could get their money back.

"What a crummy week," Oliver said when they had finally finished calling and emailing. He had grabbed a bowl full of cookies from the kitchen while Grandma was distracted trying to avoid Franz, and now everyone was munching on lemon-blueberry bars.

"It *has* been awful," Isa agreed.

"Uncle Sylvester's mom died. Papa won't be back for his big birthday celebration," Oliver said.

"Your camping trip got canceled," Hyacinth said.

"We haven't been able to talk to Papa because of the reception," Laney added.

"We're no closer to figuring out the road trip itinerary," Jessie said.

"To top it all off, Grandma has been here," Oliver said in a low voice with a shudder.

"And don't forget that terrible man at the botanical garden," Hyacinth added.

Her siblings nodded in agreement. That had been terrible.

"But there were some good things," Laney said as she petted Tuxedo.

"Like what?" Oliver said, grabbing another cookie bar and shoving it into his mouth.

"My new bike," she said. "Meeting Jamal and David and Yardsy and maybe getting to build a boat."

Isa smiled at Laney and gave her a hug. "You're right. We also learned more about Pop-Pop."

"I hate it when you look on the bright side," Oliver grumbled.

Laney went over to Oliver and put her arms around his neck. "Spin me!"

Oliver made a face, but he stood up and spun her around anyway. Laney hooted with glee.

Grandma's voice came in from down the hall. "Quit that racket! Grandpa is trying to rest!"

Oliver rolled his eyes.

"Maybe Grandma and Grandpa will leave early now," Oliver whispered as he dropped Laney onto Jessie's bed. "Since the party is canceled."

Even though they all felt a little bad about it, the Vanderbeekers brightened at the thought.

Twenty-Three

Around noon, Mama called Jessie and asked if she, Isa, and Aunt Penny could come over to the bakery. Auntie Harrigan couldn't come that day because she had a freelance job helping to build a set at a theater in Westchester. Manny was still sick, so Mama was all by herself in the kitchen.

Hyacinth watched her sisters and Aunt Penny gather their things and get ready to go. She wasn't excited to be left alone with the grandparents all day.

"Grandma, want to come to the cat café with us?" Isa asked, as if reading Hyacinth's thoughts.

Jessie shot her sister dagger eyes, which Isa ignored.

"No," Grandma said.

"Are you sure? The bakery is really cute. I think you would like it," Isa said.

"No," Grandma repeated.

"You haven't seen it before, have you?" Laney asked as she fed Paganini cilantro. "You would love it. The cats are so cute!"

"I do not want to go," Grandma said, but this time she spoke with steel in her words.

Isa raised her eyebrows at Grandma's tone. Jessie shook her head, and they left with Aunt Penny for the bakery.

Hyacinth tried to stay out of Grandma's way as much as possible for the rest of the afternoon. While Oliver went down the street to play basketball with some of his friends, Hyacinth and Laney went upstairs to have tea with Miss Josie and then to visit Orlando and Mr. Beiderman. Laney brought Tuxedo to have a kitty playdate with Princess Cutie, but they purposely left George Washington at home because he got cranky when forced to leave the apartment. It was lovely and restful being with their brownstone family, and Hyacinth felt only slightly bad that they left Grandma and Grandpa alone all afternoon.

To make things even better, Mama was closing the bakery early and coming home to make dinner. Oliver, Hyacinth, and Laney timed their return to the apartment for Mama, Isa, Jessie, and Aunt Penny's arrival. Mama got to work making special food, since it had been such a crummy day: macaroni and cheese, a salad of fresh lettuce and ripe tomatoes, potato salad with lemon and mint, and bean soup. Aunt Penny, Jessie, and Hyacinth helped get dinner ready while Isa practiced downstairs and Grandma watched and criticized Mama's food choices.

"You eat so much cheese," Grandma said, wrinkling her nose.

"There's no such thing as *too* much cheese," Oliver said as he swiped a piece of grated cheddar off the cutting board.

"I *love* cheese," Laney said as she rode by on her bike. "It's my favorite food."

"Too much is not good for you," Grandma said.

"Too much of anything isn't good for you," Jessie pointed out. "You can even get sick if you eat too much spinach."

"Paganini can't eat a lot of spinach because it has ox-lights," Laney called out from her bike.

"You mean *oxalates*," Jessie said.

"It's fine," Mama said to Grandma. "The kids eat lots of different foods."

Grandma shook her head. "And the beans? So many beans?"

Laney went by again on her bike. "I love beans! Mama gets them special from a farmer and they are delicious!"

Hyacinth kept quiet, cutting the lettuce leaves to a more manageable size and gathering the salad toppings. She really hoped Grandma wouldn't say anything to her.

"Hyacinth, you need to slice those radishes thinner! Why are you putting crackers on top? Aren't you going to shake up that dressing?" It was as if Grandma couldn't help herself, and by the end of dinner prep, Hyacinth was feeling extra frazzled. Mama tried to intervene, but Grandma would not be silenced.

Finally, the food was ready. Hyacinth made sure to take the seat farthest away from Grandma. Unfortunately, distance didn't stop her. Grandma nagged

Hyacinth to sit up straighter, to speak louder and more clearly, and to eat more vegetables and less potato salad and macaroni and cheese. The constant barrage made Hyacinth want to stop eating entirely and hide in her bedroom until Grandma went back to Ottenville.

"Can we talk to Papa tonight?" Laney asked when Grandma took a breath between reprimands.

"He doesn't have any reception," Mama said. "He had to walk to the gas station to use the landline there to call me about his canceled flight."

"I miss him so much," Laney said, and she started to cry.

Hyacinth put her arm around her sister.

Grandma shook her head disapprovingly and turned back to Hyacinth. "I hope you're not going to cry too."

"Mom," Mama said, "be gentle."

"Be gentle?" Grandma said. "No, the kids do not need more 'gentle'. You and Derek give them enough of that. They need more direction. They need to grow up and get good jobs. Not be bakers and musicians and basketball players."

There was a moment of dead silence, as if the brownstone was holding its breath.

"They are doing just fine," Mama said, her voice tight and thin.

"We love that Mama is a baker," Isa said.

"We're proud of her. She has her own business," Jessie added.

"She got reviewed by the *New York Times*," Oliver said. "They called her cookies sublime."

"They are the most delicious things in the world," Laney finished.

"You gave up accounting for baking," Grandma said to Mama, refusing to back down. "I still don't understand it."

Mama looked sad and confused and disappointed all at once, and Hyacinth felt a hot burn begin in her belly. It felt as if it would turn into a raging fire if she didn't let it out.

"*Stop* it," Hyacinth said, her voice louder than she intended. But it felt good to shout a little, as if her words had power and strength.

Everyone froze and stared at Hyacinth.

Hyacinth let her voice grow even louder. "Mama

is amazing and the best cook and baker and her food is delicious! And Papa is the best papa in the world! And you are mean and you make us all feel bad about ourselves and you never have anything good to say about anyone. And you won't go to Mama's bakery, and I think it's because you're afraid to see that Mama is following her dream. And Oliver is great at basketball and he's smart too, and Isa is the best violin player and is one day going to be the most famous violinist and tour all over Europe, and Jessie will study important science things and help the world be a better place, and I don't know what Laney is going to do but she's going to be amazing at whatever she does because she is the nicest person to ever live and gets along with everyone. So stop making us feel bad about ourselves and if you don't have something nice to say, then don't say anything at all!"

There was a stunned silence at Hyacinth's outburst. Grandma looked as if Hyacinth had just punched her, and Hyacinth instantly wished she could swallow up all those words and take them back.

"I'm sorry, Grandma," Hyacinth began, her voice quiet again.

But Grandma shook her head, standing up so abruptly that her chair toppled backward and clattered to the floor. Then she rushed out of the brownstone, shutting the front door behind her with a finality that seemed to say she would never cross the Vanderbeeker threshold again.

Twenty-Four

Hyacinth didn't know what to do. She had never lost her temper like that before, and she wanted the floor to open up underneath her so she could sink into the ground and disappear. She closed her eyes to avoid seeing the disappointed faces of her family.

She felt the light pressure of a hand resting on her shoulder, and then another one, and then more. She lifted her head to see Mama, Isa, Jessie, Oliver, Laney, Aunt Penny, and Grandpa all surrounding her.

"It's okay, Hyacinth," Mama said.

"You did good," Oliver said.

"That was very brave of you to stick up for all of us," Isa said.

"I should have said those words to her a long time ago," Mama said.

"Me too," Grandpa said.

Everyone looked at Grandpa. There was a long pause before he spoke.

"I'm sorry, Hyacinth," Grandpa finally said. "Sometimes it's easier to let things go than to confront them, and I got used to letting things go. I'm sorry."

"I need to say sorry to Grandma," Hyacinth said. "I meant everything I said, but I shouldn't have yelled at her."

"I can go with you," Mama said. "If you want."

"I wonder where she went," Laney said.

Hyacinth thought for a minute. "I think I know."

✦ ✦ ✦

Hyacinth and Mama didn't say much as they walked along the quiet streets. It was still bright outside, but even though it was a warm August evening, Hyacinth shivered. As they passed the brownstones on their street, she noticed lots of windows thrown open to let in the summer breeze. Hyacinth reached out to hold Mama's hand.

They turned north on Adam Clayton Powell Jr. Boulevard, walking by pharmacies closed for the night and bodegas still buzzing with customers buying submarine sandwiches for dinners or last-minute groceries. They turned right on 143rd Street and passed Central Harlem Animal Hospital. While it was closed, the lights were still on, and they could see Dr. Singh inside, talking to a patient holding a large bulldog in his arms.

From the corner, Hyacinth could see a solitary person standing near the middle of 143rd Street. The person was looking at a building, the twinkle lights from the storefront illuminating her silhouette. When they were a few yards away, Mama released Hyacinth's hand and Hyacinth walked by herself toward her grandmother.

"Hi, Grandma," Hyacinth said, turning so she was facing the Treehouse Bakery and Cat Café like Grandma was.

When Grandma didn't say anything, Hyacinth shifted uneasily. The shame of having yelled at her grandmother filled her mouth with a sour taste.

Hyacinth swallowed. "I'm sorry for yelling."

There was such a long period of silence after Hyacinth's apology that she wondered whether she should leave, but then Grandma spoke.

"You're right," Grandma said, "about me being afraid. I was afraid that your mom was going to be unhappy like I was. I didn't want her to wait on people and be on her feet for twelve hours every day. I didn't want her to worry about money."

"Really?" Mama interjected from behind them.

Hyacinth glanced back at Mama, then turned to Grandma. "You want Mama to be safe."

Grandma nodded. "Grandpa and I retired two weeks ago."

"You did *what*?" Mama said, but she pressed her lips together when both Hyacinth and Grandma turned to look at her.

Grandma continued. "We've worked almost every day of our lives for fifty years. And now we have nothing to do but think about lost time. The lost time with your mom and the lost time with you. I thought if we spent time together, I could fix everything. But I made it worse instead."

Hyacinth didn't know what to say to that. She

knew how difficult it was to change the way you were. "Last year Orlando helped me make new friends. It wasn't easy."

Grandma turned and looked at Hyacinth. "I think I have been hard on you because you remind me of myself when I was younger. I thought you needed to be stronger. But I was wrong about you. You are strong. You speak with a clear voice. You protect your family."

Hyacinth didn't know how to respond. She had never thought of herself as a strong person, but Grandma's words encouraged her.

She searched for what to say. "We want to know you better, Grandma," Hyacinth said.

Tears filled Grandma's eyes. "I watched you looking for information about your dad's father all week. You were so determined to find out about him. And I have been here all along and have not given you a good reason to know me."

Hyacinth didn't respond. Instead, she took Grandma's hand and led her to Mama, joining their hands together. And they stood there, three generations of strong women, holding one another's hands and forgiving one another under the darkening summer sky.

＊ ＊ ＊

Laney was already in bed when Hyacinth came home with Grandma and Mama. Isa and Jessie were sitting in bed with her because Laney didn't want to go to sleep in an empty bedroom. And Oliver was in the bedroom because he was upset about Papa's birthday party being canceled and wanted to complain about it where people could hear him.

Hyacinth entered the bedroom, her face peaceful and happy.

"Did you find her?" Jessie asked.

Hyacinth nodded. "She was at the bakery."

Oliver whistled.

"Did she like it?" Isa asked.

Hyacinth nodded. "And we talked."

"I'm glad," Jessie said. "That must have been really hard."

"It was," Hyacinth acknowledged. "But I think things are going to get better."

"That's so great, Hyacinth," Isa said, sitting up and stretching. "That took a lot a courage."

"What a weird week," Jessie said as she yawned.

"Yeah," Oliver said. "Good things and bad things, all mixed up together."

"I can't believe Papa won't be back for his party. Everyone was going to be there," Jessie said.

"No party and no present," Isa said gloomily. "So much for celebrating Papa's fortieth birthday."

Isa and Jessie got ready to go back to their bedroom, but Laney stopped them. "Let's be together for a little bit."

Isa looked at Jessie, who shrugged. "Sure," they said.

"You too, Oliver?" Laney asked.

Oliver nodded and settled back down on the carpet with Franz and Hyacinth. Isa took her phone out and put on the Bach cello suites, and they sat listening to the music, letting their minds rest from the stress of a long week. Laney was feeling drowsy and comfortable in her bed, surrounded by her blankets and stuffed animals and siblings and the lovely low notes of the cello, when she heard those familiar footsteps going down the hall. She sat up.

Oliver looked at her. "What—"

"Shh!"

Laney waited until the footsteps descended and the

door to the backyard opened and closed. "Come on," Laney said, gesturing to her siblings.

She crept down the stairs and past her sleeping mom and aunt. She led the way through the kitchen and to the back window. Grandpa was outside, and to Laney's surprise, she also saw Grandma with him. Together they moved in the moonlight, their silhouettes strong and graceful.

"Wow," Isa breathed. "I didn't know they could move like that."

"Come on," Laney whispered, and she walked to the back door.

"Maybe they want to be left alone," Hyacinth said, hesitant.

"No, Grandpa likes it when people join him," Laney insisted, and she opened the door.

Grandpa and Grandma didn't notice them come out at first, but when the door closed with a quiet click, they turned their heads to see the five Vanderbeeker kids outside. They hesitated before continuing again, and everyone tried to copy their movements except Laney, who let her body move the way it wanted to.

While Harlem slumbered, the yard behind the red

brownstone on 141st Street pulsed with life and new beginnings. Isa, Jessie, Oliver, Hyacinth, and Laney danced under the big maple tree with their grandparents, beneath the charcoal sky, surrounded by the soft glow of New York City lights.

Friday, August 8

One Day Until Papa's Birthday

Twenty-Five

The sun greeted the brownstone on 141st Street with a beautiful rise that transformed the sky into a canvas of gold and orange and pink. Unfortunately, none of the Vanderbeeker kids were awake to see it. They had all been up late, doing tai chi together in the backyard until one by one they collapsed on the grass and looked through the tree branches to see the sky. While they were staring up into the cosmos, something truly magical happened. For the first time in their lives, the Vanderbeekers heard some of Grandma's stories.

They heard how Grandma and Grandpa had left China and come to America as a newly married couple, and how they worked long hours washing dishes and running the cash register at a nearby restaurant, the same restaurant they had just retired from after forty-five years. They learned how hard it had been for them to communicate and how they had gone to English class every morning before work because they wanted to be able to speak English to the kids they hoped to have.

Then Grandpa had shared a story. On the day of their first wedding anniversary, they had to work at the restaurant. When their shift ended, Grandma and Grandpa put their aprons in the laundry, threw their hairnets away, and washed their hands. They were about to head out the back door to the parking lot when one of the cooks asked them to leave out the front because someone was hosing down the back entrance and it was all soapy and slippery.

Grandma and Grandpa didn't think much of it— that was not unusual—but when they stepped out into the dining area, they were surprised to see one of the tables set up with a white tablecloth, two candles, and a vase of roses. Two of their favorite servers, Emmanuel and Marta, led them to the fancy table and poured a bubbly pink soda into wineglasses, then served a special meal the chefs had prepared just for them. It wasn't food they normally served at the restaurant. It was food Grandma and Grandpa loved and missed from the country they'd left: crispy rice noodles and stir-fried vegetables and dumplings packed with delicious spices swimming in a flavorful broth. For dessert, there were delicate egg tarts with centers as yellow as the sun and layers of flaky pastry holding it all together.

When Grandpa finished telling that story, he looked at Grandma and said, "We should do that again."

And Grandma looked at Grandpa, smiled, and said, "That would be nice."

✧ ✧ ✧

It was nearly nine o'clock when the Vanderbeekers woke up on Friday morning. Isa blinked and her mind went instantly to the previous night. The events of the past week flooded into her memory, and she felt more connected to her extended family than ever before.

Jessie stirred, and Isa looked over and thought about how she and her siblings carried the stories of so many people.

They carried the stories of the brownstone, of Mama and Papa and of Mr. Jeet and Miss Josie and of Mr. Beiderman and Orlando.

They also carried the stories of their grandparents, and of their grandparents' grandparents.

And they carried their own stories, which they were creating each day with each other in the cozy brownstone and in their neighborhood and country and world.

The bedroom door opened, and Laney leaped inside with Tuxedo. Hyacinth and Franz were behind her.

"I slept so late!" Laney exclaimed. "And now I'm full of energy."

Tuxedo leaped onto Jessie's bed and sat on her face.

"Ugh," Jessie said, turning her head.

"We need to see Mr. Ritchie today," Hyacinth said, referring to the owner of a flower and tree stand just over the Harlem River in the Bronx. Papa had known Mr. Ritchie since he was a little kid, and they bought their Christmas tree from him every year. "He doesn't have a phone, so we couldn't tell him Papa's party was canceled."

Isa nodded. "We should do that right after breakfast."

Mama had left a note on the dining room table with a bowl of fruit and a big pile of cheese croissants from Castleman's. The note said that she had gone to the bakery with Grandma, Grandpa, and Aunt Penny. They would be back after lunch.

The Vanderbeekers dug into the croissants and fruit, cleaned up the kitchen, and headed to Mr. Ritchie's stand. Walking along 145th Street, they crossed the bridge, taking a moment to admire a group of rowers on the Harlem River. They entered the Bronx and waved when they saw Mr. Ritchie. He sat on an overturned apple crate next to his white van. A couple of folding tables were covered with flowers and plants. He nodded to the kids as they approached, his small black radio propped up next to him and playing one of Isa's favorite pieces from *Peter and the Wolf* by Sergei Prokofiev.

"Hi, Mr. Ritchie," Hyacinth said, handing him a bag with two croissants in it.

Mr. Ritchie nodded his thanks, a toothpick wedged between his teeth.

"I know you were planning on coming to Papa's fortieth birthday party tomorrow, but we have to postpone it," Isa said. "Papa went to Indiana for a funeral and his flight got canceled and he can't get home until next week."

Mr. Ritchie nodded again.

"We'll let you know when it's rescheduled," Isa told him.

Hyacinth, who had been looking at the plants, pointed to one of them.

"Is this a Cattleya orchid?" she asked.

Mr. Ritchie nodded.

"That's the one Grandma really liked," Hyacinth told her siblings. "I think we should buy it for her. I have some allowance money."

Isa looked at the price sticker.

"I have some money too," Oliver said, pulling a five-dollar bill from his pocket.

"Me too," Jessie said, reaching into her pocket for some dollar bills.

While Isa paid, she kept an eye on Laney, who was doing cartwheels on the sidewalk by Mr. Ritchie's van. She was about to say "Be careful!" when Laney got a little too close to the van and almost ran into the back bumper. But then Isa's eyes drifted over the license plate, and she froze.

Twenty-Six

Oliver was eager to get home—he was hungry again, and he knew Mama had left a container of Auntie Harrigan's ginger cookies on the counter—but Isa was taking her sweet time paying for the orchid. Now she was just staring at Mr. Ritchie's van as if it were a ghost.

"Hello!" Oliver said, waving a hand in front of her face. "Can we get going? I'm—"

"Look," Isa whispered, pointing.

Oliver looked at the van.

"What do you want me to—"

"Look!" Laney yelled as she too pointed to Mr. Ritchie's van. "His license plate says Ludwig! Just like Ludwig van Beethoven!"

"Oh my gosh," Jessie said.

Isa turned slowly back to Mr. Ritchie. "Is that van's name . . . Ludwig?"

Mr. Ritchie smiled.

"How long have you had it?" Isa said.

Mr. Ritchie pulled the toothpick out of his mouth. "'Bout twenty-five years."

Isa swallowed. "You knew our grandfather?"

Mr. Ritchie nodded.

"Is your first name Joe, by any chance?" Oliver asked, remembering the name from the letter.

Mr. Ritchie nodded.

The Vanderbeekers looked at one another.

"Was this the van our grandfather was going to use to take a road trip after our dad's graduation?" Isa asked.

The Vanderbeekers all held their breath, waiting for Mr. Ritchie to respond.

"Yes."

✧　✧　✧

Laney couldn't help it. She just had to hug Mr. Ritchie.

"We have been trying to learn more about Pop-

Pop," Laney said as she squeezed him tight, "and we found a letter he wrote to Papa and discovered he was going to surprise Papa with a road trip and we figured out where Whalers Cove was in California but we didn't know what other places they were supposed to go to and we wanted to re-create the trip for Papa but we couldn't and now I can't believe we found the actual van and it was *your* van!"

Mr. Ritchie nodded and, after hugging Laney back, stood up and walked to the passenger side of the van. The Vanderbeeker kids followed. He opened the door, leaned in, opened the glove compartment, shifted some things around, and pulled out a canvas pouch. He unzipped the pouch, removed a folded piece of paper, and handed it to Isa.

Laney watched Isa open the paper with trembling hands. There, in their grandfather's beautiful handwriting, which they had become so familiar with over the past week, was a hand-drawn map with a complete itinerary of the road trip.

Mr. Ritchie waited until they had all read the paper. Then he stepped aside and gestured to the vehicle. "He's ready when you are."

The Vanderbeekers burst into the Treehouse Bakery and Cat Café. They were shocked to see Grandpa behind the counter, wearing a bakery T-shirt and preparing coffee drinks, while Grandma stood by the cash register, taking a person's order.

"Grandma! Grandpa!" Jessie said, shocked. "What are you doing?"

Grandma's eyebrows rose. "We are working. What do you think?"

"Do you know what you're doing?" Isa asked.

Grandma frowned. "I worked as a cashier in a restaurant for forty-five years."

Grandpa held a mug aloft, as if he were toasting them. "She was the best cashier. Never a mistake. And so fast."

Grandma shook her head, but it was obvious she was pleased.

"We're going back to see Mama," Jessie told them.

"And this orchid is for you," Hyacinth said, pushing the orchid across the counter.

"We found the van!" Laney called.

The Vanderbeekers rushed down the hallway that led to the kitchen and burst through the doors. The industrial mixer was churning away, creating lots of noise.

"Mama!" they yelled.

"We got the itinerary!" Oliver added.

"Mr. Ritchie said the van is ready for us!" Isa said.

"And that means—" Jessie began.

"—that we need to go to California!" Hyacinth finished.

Mama, Aunt Penny, and Auntie Harrigan had frozen in the middle of their work. They stared at the kids.

They heard footsteps behind them, and Grandma walked in, cradling her orchid. She turned and looked at a very confused Mama. Aunt Penny stopped the mixer, and the kitchen went silent.

"The kids found a letter from Pop-Pop that he meant to give to Derek for graduation," Grandma explained. "He was going to take Derek on a cross-country trip to California right after graduation. And the kids figured out the trip so they could re-create it for his fortieth birthday present." She looked at the kids. "Did I get that correct?"

"Yes!" they said.

"How did you know?" Hyacinth asked.

"You are very loud," Grandma said. "It was easy to figure out."

"But, Mama, guess what?" Jessie continued, breathless. "We found the *exact* van Pop-Pop was going to use. It belongs to Mr. Ritchie, and he keeps his van in top shape because he used to be a mechanic—he recently replaced the engine and the tires!—and he says we can use the van for the trip! So we could go on a trip in the *exact same van* that Pop-Pop was going to use!"

"But doesn't Mr. Ritchie need his van?" Mama said, confused.

"His friend has one he can use!" Laney shouted.

"You're not saying that we should leave *today*?" Mama said.

"We *have* to leave today because we have to pick up Papa," Oliver said reasonably. "So we can be with him for his birthday."

"We need to get there by tomorrow!" Laney shouted.

"It's an eleven-hour-and-thirty-nine-minute drive, so if we start tonight, we can stay in a hotel somewhere in Pennsylvania and get there by tomorrow afternoon," Jessie said.

"We *have* to be with him on his fortieth birthday," Hyacinth said.

"But we can't just leave our home," Mama said, her eyes wide. "I have work! The bakery won't run itself."

"I can take care of the bakery," Auntie Harrigan offered. "I pretty much work here full-time anyway, with my freelance jobs being so unpredictable. I know all your recipes, and I have lots of other ideas. Who knows? Maybe I'll come up with a whole new cookie menu by the time you get back. And Manny said he was coming back to work tomorrow. We'll be fine!"

"Grandpa and I can stay at the brownstone and work the front of the bakery," Grandma said.

"But you just retired!" Mama said.

Grandma sniffed. "I do not like retirement. Better to be busy."

"What about Papa's job?" Mama asked, looking at her kids.

"He has lots of vacation time saved up!" Hyacinth said. "He told me that last week!"

"And we've been putting money in the Fiver Account all year!" Laney said, referring to their vacation fund. "That will *pay* for the trip!"

"And our pets?" Mama said.

"Franz and Tuxedo would come with us, obviously," Laney said. "They've always wanted to go on a road trip."

"We'll take care of George Washington and Paganini and . . . the chickens," Grandma said, with reluctance.

"As long as you don't eat the chickens!" Laney said.

Grandma rolled her eyes. "Of course I will not eat the chickens. They have names."

"But we *will* eat the eggs," Grandpa said, stepping into the kitchen and catching the last part of the conversation.

"I'm okay with that," Hyacinth said.

"This is nuts," Mama said, shaking her head.

"But we're going to do it, right?" Oliver asked.

Everyone looked at Mama and held their breath, waiting for her answer.

Twenty-Seven

The scene at the brownstone was positively chaotic that afternoon.

"Don't forget to turn the ovens off at the end of the day," Mama told Aunt Harrigan as she grabbed random items and threw them into a huge duffel bag. "The health inspector comes once a year—it should be in the next couple of months, but it's unannounced, so always make sure everyone in the back is wearing their hairnet, and do the cleaning regimen posted on the wall every day—"

"I know," Auntie Harrigan said. "I was around the last time you had an inspection."

Oliver emerged from the basement, dragging some camping gear.

"Oliver, do we really need all that?" Mama asked.

"Yes," Oliver grunted, then proceeded to lug a tent out the door.

"This is just nuts," Mama said, reaching into the cupboard for her emergency chocolate and shoving it into her backpack. "Mom, don't overfeed George Washington. He'll look at you as if he hasn't been fed in months, but don't give him more than one scoop of food twice a day, okay?"

"Okay," Grandma said, looking at George Washington. He was staring at his bowl sadly.

"And be sure to let the chickens out at six o'clock every morning. There's a latch you can pull from my room that will open the coop so you don't have to go downstairs—Jessie rigged it up—but you have to physically latch it when you put them back in at night, okay?"

Grandpa nodded. "We will do that."

"And be sure to open the windows when you use the stove or the oven, because the fire alarm is really sensitive, and the fire department doesn't like it when it goes off because they have to come here and—"

"Okay, okay," Grandma said, waving her hands. "Don't worry."

Grandpa raised one finger in the air. "I will fix all the leaky faucets!"

Oliver ran back inside. "I need my basketball!"

The sound of feet on the stairs revealed Mr. Beiderman and Orlando.

"Jessie just texted me. Are you really going on a road trip for a *month*?" Orlando said.

"Yes!" Laney said as she rolled her bike out the door. "We're going to pick up Papa in Indiana and then take him to California to see Whalers Cove!"

Mr. Beiderman looked at Aunt Penny. "Are you going with them?"

She shook her head. "My flight home is on Sunday morning, and I've got work on Monday. But they'll stay with me when they get to California."

Jessie, wearing Pop-Pop's blazer despite the heat, emerged from the basement with more camping equipment. "Hi!" she said when she saw them.

"I can't believe you're leaving for a whole month," Orlando said as he went to help her. "What will I do without you?"

"You should come," Jessie said. "You and Mr. Beiderman. The van is huge. There's plenty of room."

Mr. Beiderman said, "That's ridiculous," at the same time that Orlando said, "Could we, Mr. B?"

And because Mr. B was a softie around Orlando, he looked at Mama. "What do you think? I mean, I can work from anywhere, and Orlando has nothing to do until school starts up again."

Mama looked at him, then at Jessie, who was standing behind them with a big smile and both thumbs up.

"Sure, why not?" Mama said. "The van seats ten. You have to share the driving, though. *And* you have to be ready in thirty minutes, or we're leaving without you."

Jessie cheered, and Orlando sprinted up the stairs to pack.

Mr. B looked at Aunt Penny. "Looks like I'll see you in California."

Aunt Penny smiled. "Sounds good to me."

Mr. B gave her a rare smile back, then went up the stairs to gather his stuff.

"I can't believe we're doing this," Mama said.

Fifty-three minutes later, everyone was lined up on the sidewalk of 141st Street. Mr. Ritchie, Miss Josie, Aunt Penny, Grandma, and Grandpa had been helping organize the luggage and pet food and camping equipment, so it all fit in the van like a huge puzzle. Mr. Beiderman finished strapping Laney's bike to the rack on top of the van, and they were ready.

"I think that's it!" Mama said, looking at her parents.

"Be safe," Grandma said at the same time Grandpa said, "Drive safely."

Grandma looked at Mr. Beiderman. "You better be a good driver. If anything happens to them . . ."

Mr. Beiderman cut her off. "I'm a good driver."

Mama looked at Grandma. "Don't forget—"

"Don't worry," Grandma said. "Everything is fine. Have a good time. Tell Derek we said hello. I love you."

Mama immediately turned sniffly as she hugged Grandma. Then Laney hugged Grandpa. Oliver hugged Miss Josie. Jessie hugged Grandma. Hyacinth hugged Aunt Penny. Isa hugged Mr. Ritchie. Everyone was hugging everyone else until finally the Vanderbeekers and Orlando—plus Franz and Tuxedo—piled into the van and put their seat belts on. Mama climbed into the driver's seat and Mr. Beiderman got into the front passenger seat and everyone rolled down their windows.

"Good-bye!" Laney yelled. "See you next month!"

"We love you," they said back, waving and wiping their eyes. "Be careful!"

"We love you!" the Vanderbeekers said back.

Mama started the van and pulled out of the parking space. She honked the horn.

"Good-bye, brownstone!" Oliver said.

Ludwig the Van rolled down 141st Street. Laney swiveled her head so she could watch her favorite people until they became tiny specks. Then the van turned north on Frederick Douglass Boulevard, and the specks disappeared.

"Mama!" Laney said, an idea popping into her brain. "We have to stop by the bakery!"

Mama knew what Laney wanted. She exchanged a look with Mr. Beiderman; then she made a couple of turns and came to a stop in front of the Treehouse Bakery and Cat Café. She turned the engine off and jumped out of the van with Laney. A few minutes later, they emerged with Peaches and Cream in a big animal carrier.

"More animals!" Oliver grumbled, but he moved over so they could wedge the carrier at his feet.

"Meow," said Peaches.

"Meow," said Cream.

"Aaaa-rooo!" said Franz.

"Purr," Tuxedo said from her crate.

Before Laney buckled up, she took the two photos of Pop-Pop that Mrs. Castleman had given Isa and propped them up on the dashboard.

The van turned onto the avenue, weaving around potholes, leaving Harlem and rolling through Washington Heights toward the George Washington Bridge. The bridge led them across the Hudson River, and then the van pointed toward Indiana and Papa. The miles stretched before them with the promise of new adventures.

The Vanderbeekers couldn't wait.

Acknowledgments

This is the fifth book I have worked on with my wonderful editor, Ann Rider, and I always find myself in awe that I get to work with such a lovely and thoughtful human being. I am so grateful for her love for the Vanderbeekers and the brownstone on 141st Street. Thank you to Tara Shanahan, who has believed in these stories from the very beginning and does so much to share them far and wide. I could not ask for a better team at HMH. Sending love to Celeste Knudsen and Cade Kung for the gorgeous book design, Katya Longhi for another stunning cover, Jennifer Thermes for the charming map endpapers, and Catherine Onder, John Sellers, Mary Magrisso, Candace Finn, Lisa DiSarro, Amanda Acevedo, Alia Almeida,

Anna Ravenelle, Harriet Low, all of the sales reps, and Colleen Fellingham and Alix Redmond.

Ginger Clark is a gift. I'm grateful for her advice, encouragement, and advocacy. To Holly Frederick, I send a vibrant Harlem garden for being a terrific film agent. I am thankful to Nicole M. Eisenbraun and Madeline R. Travis for all their hard work and support.

Librarians, teachers, and booksellers are national treasures and deserve palaces and an endless supply of cookies. I am thankful for all the ways they share their love of reading with young people.

Hugs to Amy Poehler, Kim Lessing, Matt Murray, and the entire Paper Kite team!

One of the best parts about being a writer is being surrounded by compassionate and creative colleagues in the Kid Lit community. Special thanks to Lauren Hart and Laura Shovan for their feedback on an early draft of this book. So many writer friends have encouraged, advised, and made me laugh this year. Thank you to Sarah Mlynowski, Christina Soontornvat, Stuart Gibbs, Max Brallier, Hena Khan, Rebecca Stead, Jenn Bertman, Supriya Kelkar, Vicki Jamieson, Linda

Sue Park, Gbemi Rhuday-Perkovich, Jarrett Lerner, Janice Nimura, and Celia C. Pérez.

Lots of love to Lauren Hart, Emily Rabin, Katie Graves-Abe, Harrigan Bowman, Kate Hennessey, the Glaser family, and the Dickinson family for being wonderful, amazing people. A special shout-out to the communities that have inspired and encouraged me, including the Town School, Book Riot, Read-Aloud Revival, the New York Society Library, the Renegades of Middle Grade, the New York Public Library, All Angels' Church, and my Harlem neighbors.

I wrote this book while sheltering at home with my family during the coronavirus pandemic. Huge thanks to the health care workers and essential workers who kept us safe.

Each book I write is always possible because my family inspires and loves me. Each book is always because of and for Dan, Kaela, and Lina.

Don't Miss More Vanderbeekers Adventures!

★ "A pitch-perfect debut. . . . Highly recommended."

—*School Library Journal,* starred review

"An excellent sequel."

—*School Library Journal*

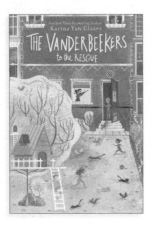

"Almost a case study in why these kinds of series are so captivating for young readers. . . . Heartfelt."

—*New York Times Book Review*

"As lovable as ever."

—*Kirkus Reviews*

And look for
The Vanderbeekers on the Road
in fall 2022!

Turn the Page for an Excerpt from Karina Yan Glaser's Poignant New Novel, *A Duet for Home*, Coming April 2022!

SUNDAY, SEPTEMBER 30

~

Days at Huey House:
Tyrell 1,275; June 1

ONE

June

CAN BAD LUCK FOLLOW A PERSON FOREVER? June Yang had always believed there was a cosmic distribution of fortune by which everyone had equal amounts of good and bad luck in their lives. But here June was, miles away from home, standing in front of a drab, used-to-be-white building with her viola strapped to her back and a black garbage bag next to her filled with everything she owned in the whole world. Her theory about luck must be wrong, because it seemed as if she had had enough bad luck for two lifetimes.

"What is this place?" asked Maybelle, her little sister.

June didn't answer. She stared up at the building. The

entrance had a crooked sign nailed over the entrance that said *Huey House.*

Maybelle, who was six years old, wore multiple layers of clothes on that unseasonably warm September afternoon: several pairs of underwear, leggings under her jeans, two T-shirts, three long-sleeved shirts, a sweater, and her puffy jacket, a scarf, winter hat, and sneakers with two pairs of socks. If she fell over, she might roll down the street and disappear forever. June admired Maybelle's foresight, though. By wearing nearly every item of clothing she owned, she had freed up room in her garbage bag for the things she really could not live without: her books (all about dogs) and stuffed animals (also all dogs).

Maybelle really liked dogs.

"Is this like jail?" Maybelle continued, poking the bristly hairs from the bottom of her braid against her lips. "Did we do something really bad? When can we go home again?"

June put on her *everything will be just fine!* face. "Of course it's not jail!" she said. "It's an apartment building! We're going to live here! It's going to be great!" Then she reached up to grab the straps of her viola case, reassuring herself it was still there.

"It *looks* like a jail," Maybelle said dubiously.

June gave the building a good, hard stare. Even though it appeared sturdy, it seemed . . . exhausted. There were lots of concrete repair patches on the bricks, and every single window was outfitted with black safety bars. The door was thick metal with a skinny rectangle of a window covered by a wire cage, just like the windows at school.

It *did* look like a jail, but June wasn't going to tell Maybelle that.

She glanced at her mom, but June already knew she wouldn't have anything to say. Mom had stopped talking about six months ago, right after the accident.

"June, where are—"

Before Maybelle could finish her sentence, the metal door of the building creaked open. A man—his head shaved, two gold earrings in the upper part of his ear, and wearing a black T-shirt—emerged and stared down at them from his great height. He looked like a guy who belonged on one of those world wrestling shows her dad would never let them watch. Maybelle shrank behind her, and Mom stood there still and quiet, her face blank and unreadable. June referred to this as her marble-statue face. Once, on a school field trip,

June had gone to a fancy museum and there was a whole room of carved marble heads, their unemotional faces giving nothing away.

"You guys coming in?" the man asked, jamming a thumb toward the building.

June fumbled in her jeans pocket for the piece of paper the lady at EAU, or the Emergency Assistance Unit, had given her. The marshall, who delivered the notice of eviction, had instructed them to go to the EAU when June told him they had nowhere else to go.

June had packed up all their stuff while Maybelle cried and Mom shut herself in her bedroom. After checking and double-checking directions to the EAU (June had had no idea what that was), she'd managed to pack their things into three black garbage bags. She told Maybelle that they were going to a new home but then immediately regretted it when her sister wanted to know all the details: Was it a house or an apartment? How many bedrooms did it have? Was the kitchen large?

That was last night. Other than a funeral home, the EAU was the most depressing place June had ever been. After filling out a stack of forms and spending the night in the EAU hallway, which they shared with three other families and buzzing fluorescent lights, June had been told by the lady in charge to come here. Staring at the building and hoping it wasn't their new home, June crossed her fingers and begged the universe to have mercy on them.

The universe decided to ignore her, because the man said, "The EAU sent you, right? First-timers?"

June nodded, but her stomach felt as if it was filled with rocks.

"I'm Marcus," he said. "Head of security here."

Security? Maybelle moved even closer to June while Mom maintained her marble-statue face.

Marcus pointed to June's viola case. "You can't bring that inside. It'll get confiscated in two seconds."

The rocks in June's stomach turned into boulders. June wrapped her fingers around the straps so tightly she could feel her knuckles getting numb. "It's just a viola," she said, her voice coming out squeaky.

"Exactly. Instruments aren't allowed."

June tried to look strong and confident, like her dad would have wanted her to be. "There's no way I'm letting you take this away from me." After all, the viola was the only thing Dad had left her. It was equal to over two years of his tip money. Even after so many months, June could picture him as if he were still with them. Dad making delivery after delivery through congested and uneven Chinatown streets, plastic bags of General Tso's chicken and pork dumplings hanging from his handlebars. Dad riding his bike through punishing snowstorms because people didn't want to leave their house to get food. Dad putting the tip money into the plastic bag marked *Viola* in the freezer at the end of every shift, his version of a savings account.

Maybelle, still hiding behind her, called out, "June's the best eleven-year-old viola player in the world."

"That's not true," June said humbly, but then she wondered if Marcus thought she was going to play awful music that drove him bananas. She added, "But I'm not, like, a beginner or anything. No one had a problem with me practicing in our old apartment. And I play classical music. Mozart and Vivaldi and Bach." She felt herself doing that nervous babble thing. "I can also play Telemann if you like him. He lived during Bach's time . . ."

Marcus's mouth stayed in a straight line, but she could tell he was softening.

After a long pause, he spoke. "I can hide it in my office, " he finally offered. "If you bring it inside and she sees you with it, she'll throw it out."

June swallowed. What kind of monster would throw away an instrument? And how could she be sure that Marcus wouldn't run off with it?

"I promise to keep it safe," he added simply.

June felt Maybelle's skinny finger stick into her back. "You're not really going to give it to him, are you?"

June never let anyone touch her instrument, ever. Maybelle had known that rule the moment June showed her the viola for the first time. But what choice did June have now? It was either trust a stranger with her viola or lose it forever.

She handed the viola case over, her skin prickling with a thousand needles of unease.

TWO
Tyrell

"HAPPY BIRTHDAY TO YOU! HAPPY BIRTHDAY TO you! *Happy birthday, dear* *unintelligible murmuring*! *Happy birthday to you!*"

Tyrell Chee looked at his best friend, Jeremiah Jones, and smirked. Jeremiah shrugged, then turned his attention back to the handful of middle schoolers from the Cressida School for Girls. The Cressidas never bothered to learn anyone's name before the birthday song. Tyrell and Jeremiah knew not to say anything about it, or even to laugh. One, because they were nice kids, okay? And two, because MacVillain would erupt like Mount Vesuvius in 79 CE (their history teacher, Ms. Koss, had told them all about how that volcano buried whole *cities*).

The Cressidas, who had their drivers bring them to the South Bronx from their fancy private school in Manhattan, had brought a birthday cake for the kids at Huey House who had September birthdays. The cake was in a pink box with a gold sticker that said *Amelie's Patisserie* in curly script and was set on a folding table that had one sad red streamer taped to the front. Tyrell liked ice cream cakes best, but nobody had asked him. A pile of presents wrapped in shiny paper sat stacked on the floor. Once the Cressidas were done singing, the little kids shrieked with happiness and nearly knocked each other over as they rushed for the gifts. Tyrell and Jeremiah, however, stayed cool. They had lived here for three years. They knew what to expect.

The Cressidas carried the stacks of presents to Lulu, who was sixteen and the only person there who looked as if she was in charge. They then migrated to a corner, where they whipped out their phones, as if major things had gone down in the ten minutes they had spent setting up this birthday party, which counted toward their community service credits. Tyrell glanced over at Stephanie, the employee who usually worked the front desk. She was supposed to be supervising but was on her phone instead, probably sending selfies to her boyfriend.

Tyrell stood there, trying to ignore the screams of the younger kids, but Jeremiah shoved his hands in his pockets and drifted over to help Lulu. Even though he never said anything about it, Jeremiah crushed on her so hard. Who could blame him? Lulu had swishy dark hair that was shiny and long. Tyrell had tried to touch it once to see what it felt like, but she'd caught his wrist and said, "Touch my hair and you die."

Anyway.

Lulu directed the little kids to sit on a faded rug with a picture of a bear in a hot-air balloon on it, and Tyrell watched Jeremiah distribute the gifts.

Tyrell and Jeremiah were like brothers. They had moved in within a week of each other, and it was like glue and paper from the start. Shared the same birthday (September 9), went to sixth grade at the same boring school a few blocks away from Huey House (M.S. 121), and loved oranges but hated bananas. Even though they were together all the time, no one ever mixed them up. Jeremiah was built like a football fullback, big and solid as a refrigerator; Tyrell was more like a basketball point guard, wiry and fast, and it was good he was fast, because he spent a lot of time running away from trouble. And though he had always admired Jeremiah's cornrows,

Tyrell's hair was too straight for that style. Ma said he got his brown skin from her and his straight black hair from his dad.

The kids ripped open the presents, screaming with joy. Then the door to the meeting room burst open and a frazzled woman with pink hair wearing a dress printed with tiny kittens stepped into the room. She carried a giant cloth bag filled with something heavy on her shoulder. The room quieted down and everyone stared at her.

"Whoa," the little kids breathed, their eyes wide.

"Ms. Hunter!" squealed the Cressidas, instantly pocketing their phones and rushing to her.

"Sorry I'm late, people," the kitten lady said, giving a tiny wave with her hand up by her ear. She pulled a handkerchief out of her pocket and dabbed at her neck, then said, "I took a wrong turn when I got off the subway. I'm Ms. Hunter, the head librarian at Cressida. Sorry I'm late. It's not easy getting around the city when you're dragging around awesomeness!" She pointed to the bag.

Tyrell exchanged an eyebrow raise with Jeremiah.

"Are you ready?" Ms. Hunter asked.

"Yes!" shrieked the little kids, jumping up from their rug spots, abandoning their gifts, and swarming her.

"Now, I have to warn you," Ms. Hunter said, putting out a hand to prevent the kids from trampling her. "This bag is filled with extremely rare, priceless, and dangerous stuff."

Whoa, Tyrell thought. *This lady is good.*

Jameel, who was six, bit his lips. "How dangerous?" he lisped through his missing teeth.

"So dangerous," Ms. Hunter said, "if Ms. Gonzalez were here, she would kick me out immediately."

"Ooh," the little kids said, glancing at each other with big eyes.

Okay, fine. So this lady was really good. In English class, they call it *building suspense*. But just as kitten-dress lady opened the bag to reveal the *rare, priceless, and dangerous* contents, the door opened again and Ms. G appeared.